A SECRET WISH

Treating Angelica's silence as a challenge, Richard was determined to bring her out of the doldrums before they reached London. For the next hour or more, he kept up a steady flow of commonplaces about the weather, the countryside they drove through and people they passed on the road. But Angelica still sat mutely staring straight ahead, refusing to respond to him.

At last tired of the sound of his own voice, Richard challenged, "I see I shall have to resort to some drastic measure to get you to speak to me. Now, what would do the trick?" He thought for several minutes; then a smile tipped his mouth. "Perhaps a kiss on those pouting lips might elicit a response?"

Angelica gasped, gazing at him with a mixture of dismay and anger. Yet within her there was also a curiosity at how his lips would feel pressed to hers. Shocked at her wanton thoughts, she snapped, "You wouldn't dare, my lord."

"Hark, the lady again speaks." The earl chuckled, then countered, "Of course I would dare, my dear. After all, did you not accuse me of being a libertine? The art of lovemaking is what we libertines excel in."

Angelica's heart hammered as she noted his gaze lingering on her mouth. She forced herself to look back to the road, wondering how the young man she knew could have changed so much and why the very thought of his kiss made her warm all over . . .

from THE WICKED EARL, by Lynn Collum

BOOK YOUR PLACE ON OUR WEBSITE AND MAKE THE READING CONNECTION!

We've created a customized website just for our very special readers, where you can get the inside scoop on everything that's going on with Zebra, Pinnacle and Kensington books.

When you come online, you'll have the exciting opportunity to:

- View covers of upcoming books

- Read sample chapters

- Learn about our future publishing schedule (listed by publication month *and author*)

- Find out when your favorite authors will be visiting a city near you

- Search for and order backlist books from our online catalog

- Check out author bios and background information

- Send e-mail to your favorite authors

- Meet the Kensington staff online

- Join us in weekly chats with authors, readers and other guests

- Get writing guidelines

- AND MUCH MORE!

**Visit our website at
http://www.zebrabooks.com**

DANGEROUS
AND DASHING

Sara Blayne
Lynn Collum
Nancy Lawrence

Zebra Books
Kensington Publishing Corp.

http://www.zebrabooks.com

ZEBRA BOOKS are published by

Kensington Publishing Corp.
850 Third Avenue
New York, NY 10022

First Printing: July, 1998
10 9 8 7 6 5 4 3 2 1

Printed in the United States of America

TABLE OF CONTENTS

THE DEVILISH DUKE

Sara Blayne

Chapter 1

"I really think it is time, Eudora, that you put a stop to Cousin Eleanor's matchmaking inclinations," Eudora Precious declared grimly to herself, just before she stepped out the fourth-story window onto the narrow ledge skirting the outside of the Earl of Bremington's Elizabethan country manor. Questioning her own sanity, she inched her way past two latched windows and around a corner before she came at last to an open window. At the sound of voices issuing from the room within, she froze, her shoulder blades pressed hard against the stone wall at her back and her eyes fixed rigidly before her.

"You, my lord duke, are the devil incarnate," breathed a woman in husky accents. "I swear you have not so much as an ounce of affection in your heart for me."

"I haven't an ounce of affection for anyone, Lady Carstairs," came the masculine reply indicative of a soulless lack of concern for the accuser. "I have never made any bones about that particular quirk in my nature."

"Or that you . . . are without . . . a *shred* of SCRUPLES," observed the lady on a crescendoing note of what sounded very like the most excruciating sort of torment. "Have mercy, I pray you, Your Grace. I cannot bear it a moment longer!"

"You not only can, but you will bear it," her tormentor heartlessly informed her. "Torture, my dearest Felicia, is but the parent of pleasure."

"That is easy for *you* to say. Heartless beast," keened the lady. "An end to it, Kerne, I *beg* you!"

Eudora, in spite of her tardy arrival at the earl's house party due to a broken wheel on her coach, had been aware the moment she'd stepped foot across the threshold that she was in unsavory environs. Although the company had already dispersed to the card rooms or the music room, or apparently anywhere one wished to go in order to pursue one's own notions of pleasure, Lord Bremington had mentioned in passing that he counted the Duke of Kerne among his male guests, along with numerous viscounts, barons, a marquis and two earls, all noted members of the Carleton set. With the ladies present, they made up a party of twenty-four.

Bremington himself, a bachelor of forty in search of a wealthy young wife with whom to set up his nursery and replenish his diminished coffers, had not hesitated to make his amorous interests in Miss Eudora Precious immediately known. Clearly three sheets to the wind, the besotted nobleman had cornered her in the foyer and again in the hall outside her assigned bedchamber. Reminding her that she was long past the first blush of youth, he informed her it was time she set aside her missish airs and allowed herself to be wooed by a man of maturity and experience before she found herself firmly ensconced on the shelf.

It had little availed Eudora to assure him that she *was* on the shelf and would stay there, thank you very much, by her own choice. More than a little obfuscated, he apparently heard not a word she said.

"Egad, but you're a pretty piece, m'dear," he had exclaimed, making a grab for her. "Put aside your teasing and say you will marry me. I promise you'll not be sorry to be my countess."

"Do not doubt I am grateful for the honor you would do me," gasped Eudora, as hastily she averted her lips from his determined assault. Faith! she thought, hardly enchanted with her newest swain. Not only was his linen neckcloth stained with what she judged to be *coq au vin rouge,* served no doubt at the dinner she had missed, but his breath was sour with wine and garlic as well. "I'm afraid, however, I must refuse, my lord. It is obvious, is it not, that we should never suit."

"Not to me, *ma petite coquine,*" Lord Bremington refuted, patently unaware that his rather ludicrous blond wig had slipped to an unseemly angle, partially baring the bald pate it was meant to conceal. "Lady Brockhurst assured me that you and I should deal extremely."

"My cousin Eleanor has repeatedly demonstrated that she has as little understanding of my requirements in a possible mate as she has of my firm conviction that I am totally unsuited to marriage," Eudora did not hesitate to inform him. "And now, my lord, if you do not immediately unhand me, I fear I shall have to resort to violent means of persuasion."

As Miss Eudora Precious was of dainty proportions, weighing in at a hundred pounds fully dressed and reaching little more than shoulder height to the earl, Bremington was hardly moved to trepidation at what must clearly have been construed as a threat. Cupping his hands about the lady's shapely posterior, he was, in fact, in the act of pressing his moist lips to her bare neck, when Eudora, deciding enough was enough, brought the high heel of her cream satin French slipper down full force on his lordship's exposed instep.

"Egad!" yelped the squire, his normally ruddy complexion going an alarming shade of grey. "My gout!"

Eudora, feeling herself perfunctorily released, bolted through the door to her bedchamber and hastily propped a chair beneath the door handle. If she had thought to have dissuaded his lordship's amorous intentions, however, she was soon to be proved sadly mistaken.

"By Jove," boomed the earl some moments later, ramming his shoulder with jarring force against the heavy oak barrier. "I do like a gel with spirit. I really must have you for my wife, you glorious little termagant."

Eudora, deciding retreat was the better part of valor and little trusting the chair to hold against a prolonged assault, had taken immediate recourse to the ledge in the hope of eluding her determined suitor. With the result that she now found herself the unwitting witness to what sounded very like another female in dread peril.

And little wonder, if Lady Carstairs was in the clutches of the Duke of Kerne! His Grace, as the lady had already pointed out, was known, *not* affectionately, as "The Devil Incarnate" by his contemporaries, and with good reason, if rumor was to be believed. The duke was notorious for two things: his disdain for all the virtues held in esteem by civilized people, and a cold heart, which had never before been touched by any of the females, too numerous to count, whom he had readily seduced and then discarded.

At the sudden blood-curdling feminine shriek issuing from the room at her back, Eudora mentally added medieval torture to His Grace's list of infamies and yielded instantaneously to benevolent impulse.

Thrusting herself through the window into the room, she prepared to lend what assistance she could.

The scene that met her astonished gaze was hardly on the order of finger screws and hot tar. Indeed, a single, frozen glance at the two in the four-poster bed was sufficient to convince Eudora the lady only required her to hastily avert her eyes and remove herself as quickly and inconspicuously as possible from the premises.

Eudora, in compliance, dropped instantly to her hands and knees and crept noiselessly across the floor to the door, her ears tingling with the unbridled sounds of pleasure issuing just over her head.

Having once achieved the hall without detection, Eudora fled at once down the servants' stairs, out the door and to the stables where she ordered her coachman to ready the coach for an immediate and hurried departure *sans* Miss Little, her lady's companion, her abigail and her trunk.

Little more than fifteen minutes later, Eudora collapsed gratefully against the squabs as the coach thundered down the drive. Her limbs trembled with reaction to the harrowing nature of her escape from the Earl of Bremington, while her cheeks yet burned at her unintentional glimpse of the Duke of Kerne in a state that could only have been described as *au naturel.*

It would seem the rumors, at least regarding His Grace's manly charms, were hardly overstated, she reflected with an unconscious smile of bemusement, as she recalled to mind an impression of wondrous firm, smooth skin beneath which the muscles rippled in such a manner as to put her in mind of Michelangelo's sculpture of *David.* And little wonder. Blessed with broad shoulders, a long back tapering to a narrow waist and a delightfully firm posterior, he was truly an extraordinarily fine specimen of the male gender. Indeed, she could no longer marvel that a man reputed to be utterly ruthless in his disregard of a woman's finer sensibilities was yet noted for his long line of feminine conquests.

The Devil Incarnate presented an aspect of manly beauty that must prove an almost irresistible temptation to females.

Oh, not to her, of course, she quickly amended. While she might admire his flawless masculine physique in a purely academic fashion, she was hardly the sort to succumb to the mere physical charms of a practiced rake. She, after all, was a woman with her sights on a higher plane of perfection. Not even one so handsome as the

Devil Incarnate could hold a candle to the cosmic beauty
of the heavenly bodies, she told herself as, firmly thrusting
aside any further contemplation of the duke, she turned
her thoughts to the more pertinent matter of her cousin
Eleanor's manipulations.

Of all Eleanor's numerous attempts to see Eudora married, this one was the most ill conceived. Surely Eleanor
had not foreseen that Bremington would attempt to ravish
Eudora in order to compromise her into marriage! No, of
course she had not. Eleanor was capable of going to
extreme measures in her matchmaking ploys, but she
would never have intentionally put her cousin in harm's
way, Eudora firmly told herself. She must assume that Eleanor had grossly misjudged the earl and the nature of his
house party when she practically coerced her into
accepting Bremington's invitation by reminding her Cornelius was due for a visit to Hardwicke Court.

Faith, Eudora groaned. She should have known better.
Even the unwelcome prospect of having her elder brother
Cornelius descend upon her with his wife Hortensia and
their five young hopefuls should not have been sufficient
to outweigh her aversion to placing herself in a potentially
compromising situation, especially one endorsed by her
cousin Eleanor.

Eudora, possessed of hair so fair as to be the color of
finely spun gold and eyes the purplish blue of violets, had
once been described by a disappointed suitor as one of
Heaven's Innocents sent to earth to instruct mere mortals
in heavenly Virtue. In the norm, she found little to enjoy
in the frivolous pursuits of the Society to which, as the
niece of the Duke of Umberly, she had been born. And
certainly she had no need of a husband, who, besides
taking it upon himself to rule both her and her fortune,
would have interfered, she did not doubt, with her one
driving passion—astronomy. Eudora would have been content to spend her entire time studying the heavens and
doing her mathematical computations. At three and

twenty, after all, she was happily unwed, independent and, thanks to her grandmama who had bequeathed her a substantial fortune, free to pursue her interests in astronomical phenomena.

She would have been free, that was, had she not had to contend with her cousin Eleanor's never-ending attempts to see her wed, she reminded herself with a grimace. That, however, was about to come to an end, Eudora vowed, even if it meant she had to ruin herself to remove her name from the lists of marriageable females to do it.

"But that is it!" she exclaimed suddenly, sitting bolt upright in the coach. "The perfect solution to my problem. A fallen woman with a fortune might look forward to becoming somebody's mistress, but she would hardly be considered a viable candidate for a wife." In the event that Eudora was ruined, Eleanor would have little choice but to give up the campaign to see her cousin married.

"Yes, but it must be carefully done," Eudora reflected, ever of a practical nature. "There would be little point, after all, in going to all the trouble of getting oneself ruined if the end result turned out to be a wedding—especially a wedding with a man one could not countenance."

Sitting back once more, Eudora applied her considerable intellect to the problem before her. Obviously, she could not ruin herself with just any man. Only a gentleman without a shred of scruples would do. A man burdened with a sense of honor, after all, would very likely feel compelled either to reject her proposal outright or to insist on marrying her upon *un fait accompli,* neither one of which would do. He must, furthermore, be pleasing to look upon, nice in his personal habits of hygiene—she recalled with an involuntary shudder Bremington's deplorable lack in that area—and possessed of a modicum of intelligence in case any unexpected complications should result from the union. Any offspring, after all, would naturally accrue to her, she reflected, not entirely displeased at the prospect. While Eudora found little to recommend in playing auntie to her brother's numerous offspring and though the last thing she might wish was a husband, she had ever entertained a purely feminine desire to experience motherhood. And what better way to achieve such an end— without the complication of a husband? she mused.

The man she chose for this most delicate of matters must, therefore, be perfectly agreed ahead of time that this would be a liaison of extremely short duration, preferably one night only, and that after achieving the desired end, there would be no further need of communication between the two parties. The last thing Eudora could wish was to find herself pursued by the gentleman. Very likely that would only be trading one untenable situation for another.

Hardly had she finished detailing her criteria for the ideal candidate than it struck her she had just described with unerring accuracy none other than the Devil Incarnate.

A small, unwitting thrill, which she attributed to the chill night breeze, coursed through Eudora. But of course, she told herself. The Duke of Kerne was the ideal candidate. Indeed, she doubted not that she could find no better man for the job!

Chapter 2

Sylvester Kane, the tenth Duke of Kerne, felt an all too-familiar sensation creeping over him as he sipped his brandy and watched his newest inamorata pull rose silk stockings up over her long, shapely legs. Felicia, Lady Carstairs, was undeniably a beauty of the first water. She was, moreover, particularly well adept in bed. Unfortunately, it was only a se'ennight since he first sampled her delights at Bremington's house party, and he was become keenly aware she had already begun to pall on him. But then, he had yet to find a woman who could hold his interest longer than it took for him to become intimately acquainted with her.

A pity, he thought with a cynical twist of his handsome lips. With Felicia he had entertained hopes of a somewhat longer alliance. Besides her obvious physical attributes, she was a wealthy widow who enjoyed her singular freedom to take her pleasures with whomever she wished. On the surface, she would seem the ideal mistress. That she was also given to flights of temper, had never broadened her interests to include anything more intellectually stimulat-

ing than the latest dress fashion, or rumor of a scandalous
nature, and that she had the annoying habit of twittering
when she laughed should not have signified, since his
interests were purely of a lustful nature. The truth was,
however, he found her a dead bore out of bed, a circumstance that increasingly detracted from his pleasure in her
company. Indeed, he was acutely aware he could not summon even so much as a tepid anticipation at the thought
of lingering for a midnight supper with the beautiful Lady
Carstairs.

Recognizing all the signs, His Grace set the glass aside
and, rising, proceeded to don his coat in preparation of
taking his leave of the lady. There would be no more trysts
with the fair Felicia, as delightful as she was in bed. He
preferred to end an alliance before it reached the final
stages of disintegration. He found little to recommend in
spiteful, disenchanted females, after all.

Twenty minutes later, the duke, arriving at his town
house at the unprecedented hour of midnight, stood idly
in the foyer sifting through the pile of calling cards and
invitations that had accumulated that afternoon on the
silver salver.

One, written in a neat, flowing hand, did not fail to
catch his immediate attention. Unfamiliar with the script,
he raised the missive speculatively to his nose to inhale
the subtle scent of lilacs. A woman, obviously, he mused,
but a very young woman, lacking in sophistication. Lilac
was the scent an innocent would choose. He made as if to
toss the letter aside, then unaccountably changed his mind.
It might prove an interesting departure from jasmine and
"eau d'ange," he speculated, thinking how quickly the fair
Felicia had palled on him. Kerne tossed aside the rest of the
stack of correspondences and unfolded the lilac-scented
vellum.

The invitation, for so it proved to be, would seem
strangely at variance with the ambience of innocence he
had formulated in his mind. It requested the favor of His

Grace's attendance at Number 5 Notting Hill Square, Kensington, at an hour which, upon checking his pocket watch, he ascertained to be less than forty-five minutes away, for the purpose of witnessing an event of astronomical interest, the opportunity for which would not present itself again for another 3.3 years.

The devil, mused the duke, with the arch of an arrogant eyebrow. If the lady had meant to arouse his curiosity, she had succeeded admirably. Certainly, 3.3 years would seem an odd sort of time frame for . . . what? Kerne shrugged, unable to resolve the conundrum. Intriguingly, the lady promised His Grace would find the experience not only uniquely entertaining, but possibly to his singular advantage. It was signed, "Lady in Waiting."

The duke's immediate suspicion, that the lady must be either an eccentric or a scheming young miss foolish enough to think she might entrap him, served only to further whet his curiosity. He did not as a rule interest himself in innocents, especially very young females who were ignorant of the rules of dalliance. In general, he considered bedding virgins vastly overrated. In addition to lacking experience in the art of love, they were far too apt to confuse a man's physical appetites for something of a sentimental nature.

More intriguing, still, was the lady's address. Notting Hill Square in Kensington stood on high ground and was surrounded by large landed mansions belonging to those of the very highest rank of society, a circumstance that had earned the Campden Hill district the sobriquet of "the Dukeries." Besides the Duke of Umberly's Hardwicke Court and Kerne's own Cravenhurst, which he seldom occupied, Campden Hill boasted Campden House, which had once housed Queen Anne; Thornwood Lodge; Moray Lodge and Aubrey House, among numerous others. The mysterious "Lady In Waiting," it would seem, was of a noble pedigree indeed, mused the duke, his curiosity growing by leaps and bounds.

Young unmarried females of the most prestigious families in England did not make assignations with the Devil Incarnate. Not if they wished to keep their reputations intact. Having come into his father's title at the tender age of fifteen, he had found himself early on the object of the matchmaking ploys of particularly artful females with hearts of jade. While he had managed to escape the clutches of Parson's Mouse Trap, he had not gone unscathed. He had come away from the experiences with a disdain for all the virtues held in esteem by society and with the conviction that all females were by nature scheming, deceitful creatures to be used and discarded, but never to be trusted. At three and thirty, he had never allowed a woman access to his well-protected heart, which was forever hardened against the finer emotions, nor had he hesitated to make it known that he spurned the conventions that would have bound him to marriage for the sake of honor or for any other sake. He was rightfully judged dangerous, a law unto himself, a hardened rakeshame, a devil incarnate.

He began to reassess his estimation of the lady. It was far more likely she was already married, probably to a wealthy peer of advanced years. Young, naive, and romantically inclined, she had very likely conceived the notion of a brief dalliance in order to relieve the emptiness of a marriage of convenience. It was a familiar scenario, one to which he had not lent himself in the past several years, finding little to amuse in disillusioned brides from the ranks of the infantry. Still, the chit had managed to prick his interest, and it was true he had nothing better to do at the moment. Turning on his heel, he rang for his carriage.

Number 5 Notting Hill Court proved to be as singular as the written invitation that had lured the duke there. Built in the style of a cruciform tower with stepped sides and roofing, gables and cupola, and rising to a lofty five stories, the greystone house literally towered above its neighbors. Kerne, viewing from the curb the monstrosity of architectural design, featuring pointed arched windows of stained glass across the front, could not but be put in mind of a Gothic cathedral, an impression that was further intensified upon being admitted into a high-vaulted central hall, which, running the entire length of the structure, appeared to give an unimpeded view to the topmost story just beneath the cupola.

"The mistress is expecting you, Your Grace," intoned the butler, relieving the duke of his curly brimmed beaver, many-caped greatcoat and gloves. "Indeed," he added with a judicious air, "if I may be so bold, Your Grace, might I suggest you step over here. Am I not mistaken, Miss Precious is at this very moment descending."

Kerne, simultaneously with becoming suddenly aware of a distant rumble and clank and stepping next to the butler, tilted his head back to follow the superior servant's gaze ceilingward—to behold, descending from a skylight in the atrium roof directly overhead, what gave every appearance of being a celestial visitor dressed in a white satin evening gown.

"Your Grace," exclaimed the vision in white, as, coming to earth, she removed her daintily shod foot from a loop in the rope with which, by means of a system of counter-weights and pulleys, she had lowered herself. A hand extended, she strode forward to greet her guest, who was studying her with a peculiarly fixed intensity. "I am so glad you have come. I confess I was not at all certain you would."

Kerne, finding himself gazing into eyes the deep blue of violets and set in a face the pink and ivory perfection of an angel's, could only wonder if he were caught up in some sort of bizarre dream, the result, no doubt, he mused cynically, of the *terrine de campagne* he had sampled earlier at Lady Villier's soiree.

Immediately, he caught himself. Careful, he mentally chided. The lady, counter to his expectations, was single, past the first blush of youth and therefore up to something.

Still, she demonstrated an originality of thought and style that might make for a stimulating interlude, if nothing else. At the very least she should be taught a lesson in the dangers of flirting with the devil, he vowed, closing strong fingers about her proffered hand.

"I am of the opinion I should not have missed such an entrance for the world, Miss ... er ... Precious, is it?" responded the duke, graciously saluting the knuckles of that small, shapely member.

"Miss Eudora Precious, Your Grace," Eudora supplied, dropping into a curtsey. Rising, she favored him with a deliberate, penetrating glance that, far from demonstrating the smallest sign of trepidation in his august presence, rather gave the distinct impression this impertinent little upstart was coolly assessing his character. "We met once before, though I daresay you would not remember it. I was eighteen at the time, and you were a guest at Umberly. My grandfather, the duke, presented me to you, no doubt with the hope that you might form an attraction to me. Fortunately, you hardly noticed me."

"Fortunately?" murmured His Grace, quizzically arching a single black eyebrow. Miss Precious, it would seem, was as disarmingly frank as she was disturbingly beautiful. A rare combination in a female, thought the duke, if it were not all a guise. "Was I so very distasteful to you, then?"

"Not at all, Your Grace. You know perfectly well that you could hardly be that. I daresay there is not a woman alive whom you could not charm if you put your mind to it. I said 'fortunately' because at the time I was far too young to have known better than to lose my heart to you."

"I see," mused His Grace, the handsome lips curving ever so slightly in a smile that was distinctly ironic. "Having taken a year or two to mature, you now consider yourself safe from my unwholesome influence, is that it?"

Eudora's marvelous eyes lit most enchantingly with sudden humor. "I sincerely hope so, Your Grace," she assured him, smiling gravely. "I am, in fact, depending on it. After all, I am three and twenty now, long past the age of girlish sentiment. You may be sure, nevertheless, that I have not forgot you are the Devil Incarnate."

"Very wise of you, Miss Precious," said the duke, an odd sort of gleam in his exceedingly hard blue eyes. "Why, I wonder, do I have the presentiment that *you*, on the other hand, loom as an 'Angel of Destiny'?"

Eudora, gazing up into the chiseled countenance, inexplicably felt a chill explore her spine. Indeed, she could not but be aware that the tall, masculine figure exerted a powerful influence on her internal organs, her blood circulation and, if she were not mistaken, her temperature, which, alarmingly, appeared to be climbing. Faith, but he was a handsome devil! The high, broad forehead and long, straight nose, the prominent cheekbones and lean, firm jaw, not to mention the sensuous lips, which had a disturbing tendency to curl ever so slightly in a manner that was cynically mocking, all appeared hewn by a master craftsman, who had not failed to add for good measure a sensuous crease in either cheek. And as if that were not all or enough, His Grace had been granted hair the color of ebony and eyes like cold blue glints of steel beneath heavily lashed, drooping eyelids. Unaccountably, she found herself wondering what had happened to him to render those marvelous features peculiarly hard and reputedly soulless.

"I am hardly an angel, Your Grace. Indeed, I daresay you will think I am something quite different when you learn why I have asked you here. Not that it signifies what you think of my character. I can only hope that you do not find me entirely unattractive."

Unattractive? marveled His Grace, wondering what the devil she was after. She must be perfectly aware that she was a diamond of the first water. More than that, a man would have to be blind not to see at once that Miss Eudora Precious embodied the sweet seductiveness of innocence and beauty in a form that must clearly have been wrought by the gods for the sole purpose of inflaming a man's primitive passions. She was the sort of female men envisioned as the idealized mate they never really thought to actually encounter in this world, and when they did, they did not make her their mistress. They married her. That *he* had encountered her and under exceedingly curious circumstances was more than sufficient to set the Devil Incarnate on his guard.

"Suffice it to say that I do not find you in the least difficult to look upon. Before I commit to more than that, however, I believe I should like to know what you had in mind when you sent me your admittedly intriguing invitation. Tell me," he added, "is it your customary practice to swoop down out of the heights to greet your guests, or was your remarkable entrance staged purely for my benefit?"

"Oh, dear," exclaimed the surprising Miss Precious, her eyes widening with consternation. "I nearly forgot. I'm afraid we must hurry if we are not to be too late. I promised you an experience of astronomical interest, and the optimum time for viewing is nearly upon us. I suggest we take the stairs, Your Grace. While the rope-and-pulley is the easiest way to descend when one is in a hurry, it is rather more cumbersome going up."

Some few minutes later, having climbed five flights of stairs, the duke, panting a little from his recent exertions, found himself being ushered into the cozy confines of the cupola at the top of the house in which, to his astonishment, he discovered a rather impressive telescope mounted on a turntable at the center and trained outward with the obvious intent of viewing the heavens.

"There, Your Grace, if you please," pronounced Eudora, who, having sighted the telescope, moved away to allow the duke access to the eyepiece. "I give you Eudora I, which I first had the honor of spotting a little more than three years ago from the tower room at Umberly. Actually it was twelve hundred days, to be rather more exact. By tracing previous recorded sightings, I calculated that it follows an orbit that brings it into visual contact with earth every 3.3 years. I have been in absolute suspense ever since to discover if my calculations were correct. And there it is, precisely on time! Did you ever see anything more magnificent?''

The duke, having bent down to look through the eyepiece, was given to see with spectacular clarity the head and gleaming tail of a comet. Speculatively, he glanced up at Eudora. "No, it is truly an astronomical event."

Eudora, meeting his eyes across the telescope, went suddenly still.

"I did promise it would be, Your Grace," she replied, aware that her heart was behaving in a most erratic manner beneath her breast. "Somehow I knew you would appreciate it. Not many do, you know. I'm afraid I am thought to be something of an eccentric in my pursuits."

Eccentric was hardly the word to describe what she was, thought His Grace, taking in the lovely countenance, flushed just then with the pleasure of her achievement. *Original,* undoubtedly, or *singular,* most assuredly, and even those were not enough. He had the peculiar feeling that he had not the words for what Miss Precious was.

"You are a student of astronomy, Miss Precious?" he queried, gazing once more through the telescope, while he subdued the sudden, nearly overwhelming temptation to take her in his arms. Whatever else she might be, she was clearly an innocent ripe for the plucking. Obviously, Miss Precious was a rare phenomenon indeed. Unaccountably, he felt an unwonted aversion to taking advantage of her obvious vulnerability.

"Not a student, precisely, Your Grace," Eudora replied, leaning her hands against the window frame and gazing out at the comet, which was visible to the naked eye as a small, but bright, shimmer of light, trailing stardust in its wake. "I fancy myself an astronomer. Would it surprise you to learn that I have published papers in various academic journals? Well, only two, actually, but I am only just beginning.''

"Somehow it does not surprise me in the least, Miss Precious," replied the duke, who was beginning to realize that, while there might be a deal that was astonishing about Eudora Precious, nothing about her could ever surprise him.

In his assessment of this particular female, however, he was soon to be proven far short of the mark.

"What I do find curious is that you should have chosen me to share your moment of triumph," ventured the duke, relinquishing the telescope. "I find it difficult to believe our one brief encounter should have made such an impression on you as to merit tonight's invitation. What is it, precisely, Miss Precious, that you want from me?"

"But that is easy, Your Grace," declared Eudora, unconsciously straightening her shoulders as she met his gaze, as glittery and cold as the frozen particles of the comet. "I want you to relieve me of my maidenhead."

Chapter 3

"Dear, I have shocked you, have I not?" said Eudora, considerably taken aback at the duke's suddenly rather fixed expression. "I did warn you you might think differently about me. You needn't worry, however, that I entertain any designs on you beyond sharing a single night with you for the purpose I have just stated. I promise I do not."

"The purpose," the duke repeated in measured tones as though to make certain he had heard her correctly, "of relieving you of your maidenhead."

"Precisely, Your Grace," Eudora answered, applauding his perspicacity. "My maidenhead and my reputation for Virtue Inviolable. You cannot imagine what a burden they have both become to me or what it means to be idealized as a Bastion of Virginity. It has become utterly impossible for me to continue in my present state."

"A hideous prospect," agreed Kerne with a sober mien, upon which Miss Precious fairly beamed on him with approval.

"I am glad you understand, Your Grace. Somehow I

thought you might. I sensed at once that you are a man of powerful intellect.''

"In spite of my other . . . er . . . shortcomings,'' the duke replied humbly, "I believe I am not without a reasonable grasp of things. Still, I have yet to perfectly apprehend why you have enlisted my aid in what to others of a lesser understanding might seem at the very least an ill-conceived notion.''

Eudora shrugged. "But I should have thought it was obvious, Your Grace. So long as I am a single female of impeccable reputation, I remain a viable candidate for every bachelor in search of a wealthy wife to bear his heirs and add to his coffers. From the event of my eighteenth birthday, I have found myself the object of ceaseless attempts to woo or entrap me into marriage, when all I have ever wished is to be left alone to pursue my passion for astronomy. Is that too much to ask, Your Grace?''

The duke, who found a deal to question in the lady's preposterous line of reasoning, had the answer to at least one of his questions: why she should have chosen him for the honor. If it was to be a matter of deflowering a virgin and her reputation, who better, after all, than the Devil Incarnate? Strangely, he found little to amuse in the notion of being used as an agent of seduction.

"No more than what you would ask of me,'' he pointed out with an absurd sense of outraged sensibilities. The devil, he thought with a cynical appreciation of the absurdity of his position. Next he would be turning down an offer that did, after all, have certain obvious compensations. Clearly his sanity was in question. "Has it not occurred to you that there are other, less extreme methods of achieving solitude?''

"You mean I might enter a nunnery, or barricade myself in my house in the country until I am clearly past the age of inciting anyone to thoughts of marriage?'' posed Eudora in such a manner as left little doubt he had slipped somewhat in her estimation. "Really, Your Grace, I said I wished to be left alone. That does not mean I desire to be confined to a prison cell. Besides, you haven't the slightest notion of what my matchmaking relatives are capable. Only a se'ennight ago I found myself, at the instigation of my cousin Eleanor, clinging to the fourth-story ledge of a house to escape the clumsy advances of one of my would-be suitors, who was determined to compromise me into marriage. A few weeks before that I was pursued by a besotted lord intent on carrying me off to Gretna Green, and all because my cousin Eleanor let it drop that I rather liked a man who was not afraid to show a little initiative. I am bullied and browbeaten by my elder brother Cornelius, who feels there is something wicked about a female with a fortune who has no wish to give it or herself over to the superior guidance of a husband. Why, he even had the gall to suggest I marry my cousin Felix just to keep the fortune in the family. I daresay he would stop at nothing to see me legshackled. And all because my grandmama saw fit to leave her fortune to me that I might pursue whatever life I might choose. Now, do you see why I conceived the notion of asking you here tonight? I am offering you a rare opportunity to perform a noble deed, Your Grace. Clearly, I shall never be truly free until I have been properly ruined.''

His Grace, confronted by an idealized representation of Virtue with heaving breasts and eyes that shone huge and luminous against the ivory pallor of her face, was a deal closer to revelation than he had been before. Indeed, he was acutely aware that Miss Eudora Precious was one of those rare females who aroused with her mere presence the primitive male urge to possess and protect. Little wonder that some poor, besotted suitor had chased her out onto a ledge in his frenzied desire to compromise her into marriage. A mere mortal of the masculine persuasion hardly stood a chance against the seductive allure of a Bastion of Feminine Virginity.

But then, he was the Devil Incarnate. She had not the

least notion what she was inviting. It occurred to him that it was time she was given some inkling of the man with whom she was dealing.

"I not only see your dilemma . . ." Lightly, he clasped her wrist and drew her to him with a sudden, unerring deliberation that made her heart leap to her throat. ". . . I find I am disposed to render what service I can in your behalf."

"I am sure I cannot thank you enough, Your Grace." Eudora stifled a gasp as she felt the palms of his hands travel with tantalizing slowness up her bare arms. "Indeed, you are all kindness." It was all she could do not to shudder with the unexpectedly pleasurable sensations that seemed to flow in the wake of the Devil Incarnate's touch.

"I suggest you do not thank me yet." With a fingertip, he lightly traced the delectable contour of her cheekbone, then along her jaw and down to the tantalizing throb of her pulsebeat at the base of her neck. "And I am never kind, Miss Precious. Remember that."

"Eudora. Call me, Eudora, Your Grace," she whispered.

A smile, distinctly ironic, touched the corners of the duke's lips as, her eyes partially closed, she allowed her head to loll to one side, her senses acutely attuned to his feather-light explorations. Continuing his titillating journey round to the back of her neck and downward between her shoulder blades, he began to undo the tiny pearl buttons at the back of her white satin evening dress.

Only then did her eyes widen with sudden, startled comprehension. "Your Grace?" she blurted, her voice, to her dismay, a deal higher than normal and more than a little fraught with breathy overtones. Furiously she blushed. "Does this mean that . . . ?"

"That I am going to seduce you," Kerne finished for her. "It is what you said you wanted."

"Yes, but here—now—in the cupola?"

The corner of the duke's lips twitched ever so slightly. "How not? It is why you lured me here, is it not, Eudora?"

he lightly queried, slippi
gown down over her shou
he looked into her eyes. "Unle
second thoughts?"

Eudora, who found herself prey
thoughts, none remotely close to second
shook her head. "On the contrary, Your G

"Sylvester," interrupted the duke. A single,
eyebrow arched toward his hairline. "You did indica
you not, that we should dispense with the formalities?

Eudora swallowed. "Sylvester . . ." She had determinedly
obliged him. In the faint glimmer of starlight, Eudora
could not mistake the satirical gleam in his eyes. And then
it came to her. He *expected* her to cry off. Indeed, everything
he had done had been meant to scare her off. Suddenly,
a warm wave of gratitude washed over, even as any lingering
doubts she might have entertained were instantly banished.

"How very generous you are!" she exclaimed, awarding
him a look that fairly took his breath away. "Not at all as
I had been led to believe. You may be certain that I am
perfectly ready to be seduced by you." As if to give him
the proof of the pudding, she deliberately slipped her arms
out of her sleeves, so that she stood, gloriously bared to
the waist, before him. "Pray do not let it trouble you that
I am inexperienced in these matters," she added, no doubt
in the way of encouragement. "Try to think of it as I
do—as a noble act for which I shall always be grateful."
Unconsciously she leaned toward him, her lips parting as
if of their own accord.

Inexperienced? thought Kerne wryly, presented with an
unimpeded view of her undeniable feminine attributes.
She had been born knowing how to arouse a man's primitive passions without even trying. Egad, and yet she had
not the slightest notion of the effect she was having on
him! More than that, she presented an aspect of simplicity
and unassuming innocence that was as devastating as it

veritable angel

that returned his

ity of his motives

cribed as a wholly

e uncanny premoni-

ody damned equiva-

of a precipice. The

ead to hers.

dora, giving vent to a

against him.

ts and energies to the

pursuit ____ dies, Eudora had not

expended much ____ ing the nature of male-

female relationships. Consequently, she was hardly pre-

pared as the duke's mouth covered hers and his tongue

thrust between her invitingly parted lips to experience the

keening thrill that shot through her core or to feel her

knees go suddenly weak beneath her. At first it came to

her to wonder if she were coming down with something.

Then he released her lips to kiss with a slow sensuality her

eyes, her cheek, the corner of her mouth and, finally, her

lips again, and she knew the sudden onset of giddiness,

not to mention the frantic beating of her heart, were due

not to the ague, but to Kerne's masterful manipulations.

It was a sublime awakening to the power of her own body

to transport her to regions she had never imagined before,

and she owed it all to the Devil Incarnate.

In wonder and gratitude, she exerted herself to return

in some small measure the priceless gift of enlightenment

with which he had favored her. With a glorious sense of

abandonment, she plunged her own tongue into the moist

depths of his mouth. She was rewarded with a groan that

seemed torn from the very core of him. Alarmed, she

pulled away.

She was hardly reassured to look into the smoldering

heat of eyes only partially exposed between slitted eyelids.

the short puffed sleeves of her

s. His hands stopped, and

f course, you are having

any number of

oughts, firmly

e, I—"

rrogant

did

Indeed, she could not be mistaken in thinking that he was in the throes of some terrible anguish, and somehow she was responsible for it. "Sylvester, you are ill!" She leaned against him, her hand reaching to check his forehead for signs of fever, only to suddenly freeze in consternation as her hip came up against the hard bulge of his manhood. "Faith, what have I done?" she blurted on a ragged gasp of air, her eyes wide with bestartled wonder.

His lips twisted in a wry grimace of a smile. "Nothing, Eudora, that was not inevitable. You are a beautiful, desirable woman."

"Am I?" She lifted questioning eyes to his. "I have never seen a man's crowning glory. I wonder, Sylvester—would it be too much to ask if I . . . ?"

It came to him that matters were not progressing at all as he had expected, as, steeling himself not to flinch, he watched her kneel before him to undo the fastenings at the front of his breeches. But then, Eudora Precious was not the usual run of untutored females. Upon beholding his splendidly erect member, gloriously freed from its confinement, she uttered a low gasp of sheer admiration.

"But how magnificent you are, Sylvester!" The Devil Incarnate was hard put not to utter a groan as, with unabashed wonder, Eudora reached out to stroke his superb example of manhood. "If you must know, I have never been sure I was the sort to excite a man to passion. My brother Cornelius has been used to tell me I am an exceedingly tiresome creature whose 'demmed obsessions' with intellectual nonsense would freeze the lustiest gentleman's primitive urges."

"Your brother Cornelius sounds a remarkably stupid man," pronounced the duke in wooden tones, as beads of sweat broke out on his forehead. "Obviously, he knows nothing about you. It was clear to me from the very first that you are a woman of great passion."

Eudora gazed doubtfully up at him. "Now, you are roasting me. I am in the norm the most temperate of creatures."

"Are you?" Lifting her to him, he cupped his hand about the soft swell of her breast. A smile, distinctly satanic, flickered over his lips at her sharply indrawn breath. "You are really quite remarkable, Eudora," he murmured, inscribing a circle about her nipple with the pad of his thumb. "I believe I have never met a female with a greater proclivity for arousing a gentleman's primitive urges—or . . ." With his fingertips, he gently squeezed the nipple, already rigid with arousal. ". . . for demonstrating a more remarkable aptitude for unbridled passion."

A melting pang of pleasure burst somewhere in Eudora's nether regions. Shuddering, she arched away from him, her fingers digging into his shoulders. "Indeed," she gasped, "I believe I begin to see an endless range of possibilities I had never imagined before." And, truly, not all the ineffable beauty of the stars in the heavens had prepared her for the unfathomable wonders of her own body to which the Devil Incarnate was awakening her.

"But of course you do," applauded Kerne, marveling at her receptiveness. She was all sweet fire in his arms, was the remarkable Miss Precious. Indeed, he had never before encountered a female who so readily responded to his lovemaking. He had meant only to teach her a lesson. Instead, she inflamed his senses, deprived him of all rationale. The devil, he thought. Spanning her waist with his hands, he lifted her to the table.

Eudora gave a startled gasp. But even finding herself perched on the edge of the table, the telescope at her back, and the Devil Incarnate in the process of working the hem of her skirt up over her stockinged legs was nothing compared to the shock of surprise that went through her as his hand, exploring the silky flesh of her inner thigh, arrived at the intimate, moist heat between her legs.

"Sylvester . . . ?" came on a keening sigh.

Kerne, glancing up into Eudora's eyes, wide with startled discovery, suffered a pang of guilt mingled with a heady sense of wonder at her capacity for unbridled passion. To

say she was a precocious subject hardly did justice to Miss
Precious. Already, the petals of her body were swollen with
need, the sweet nectar of her arousal flowing in readiness
for him. He groaned, painfully aware that the primitive
passions *she* incited in *him* were of an equally unexpected
intensity. Egad, he thought, his every muscle strained. His
primitive masculine urges threatened at any moment to
snap the frayed remnants of his self-control! "Softly,
child," he uttered hoarsely, thinking, no doubt, to soothe
the trepidations natural to an Innocent. "There is nothing
to fear in what I am doing."

"I am not a child," Eudora did not hesitate to inform
him on a gusty breath. "And I am not afraid. I am . . .
overwhelmed." She shuddered with rising ecstasy, her
whole being focused on the marvelous things he was doing
to her with his fingers. "Faith, I never dreamed there
was such exquisite pleasure in ruination. My dearest, most
generous duke, pray do not stop, I beg you! I believe we
are very near *un fait accompli!*"

The duke, spreading wide her thighs, was in the process
of inserting himself between them, when her impassioned
plea, accompanied, as it was, with a wholehearted, uncondi-
tional surrender to the powerful sensations swelling toward
some glorious, final release, served, perversely, to bring
him, reeling, to his senses.

The devil, he thought, his teeth clenched against his
unbearable need to plunge his shaft into her. It was one
thing to seduce a female and walk away, quite another to
be seduced by one, especially by one who presented an
aspect of angelic innocence and a reasoning process that
was questionable at best. Eudora Precious had not the
slightest notion of what it would mean to be ruined by
anyone, much less by the Devil Incarnate. For the first
time since he had hardened his heart against all scheming
females, he discovered a repugnance at wantonly despoil-
ing the epitome of Virtue Inviolable.

He would complete the demonstration of just what Miss

Precious might have enjoyed at his hands, and then he would leave her with that as a reminder that no one presumed upon the Devil Incarnate.

Eudora writhed in the grips of what gave every promise of being a revelation of astronomical proportions, and, still, she was aware that something crucial was missing. Indeed, it was not at all as she had envisioned it to be. Surely, it took the full participation of both parties if she were to be properly ruined?

"Sylvester," she gasped, her eyes pleading. "I . . . really think . . . you had . . . better hurry. Faith, I feel I shall die if you do not *do* something."

Even in her delirium of unbearable need, Eudora could not fail to see the satirical gleam in the duke's eye. "You are not going to die, Miss Precious, I promise. You are, in fact, about to learn the power of your own body to transport you to a state of ecstasy. And that, I'm afraid, is all that I am prepared to grant you."

And, in truth, just then, when she was feeling rather like a tea kettle on the point of spouting its lid, the duke pressed the heel of his hand against her swelling bud of desire.

It was too much for her. She cried out in a shuddering explosion of release. Wave after wave of exquisite pleasure ripped through her, leaving her dazed and weak in the aftermath of her stupendous discovery. Not only was she a female of great passions, but she knew beyond any shadow of a doubt that she was anything but the Ice Maiden her brother was fond of calling her. But then, she doubted not that she owed that unexpected bonus to the Devil Incarnate's singular gifts at arousal.

Clearly, he was the master of seduction that he was reputed to be. Save, that was, for one indisputable omission—he had yet to relieve her of her maidenhead. Ignorant as she might be of male-female relationships, she was very nearly certain one could not be considered properly deflowered until the maidenhead had been broken by a man entering into her. While she could not be wholly positive, somehow she could not think the glorious manipulations to which she had been treated amounted to quite the same thing.

It was, consequently, with a sense of bewilderment that she felt him disengage himself from her, and, painfully setting himself to rights, favor her with a mocking salute.

"It has been interesting, if nothing else, Miss Precious," he observed cynically, refastening the front of his breeches. "I wish you well with your projects, both astronomical and sociological—not, however, with my further involvement. I advise you to reconsider your determination to remain single, especially by means of ruining yourself. If you have learned anything from this night's events, it should be that you are obviously a female who would benefit from marriage to a young, virile male. And, now, I shall bid you goodbye, my dear, with the hopes that we shall not have cause to meet again. I promise you will not escape so easily if ever again you place yourself in my power."

"But, Sylvester," exclaimed Eudora, oblivious to her state of extreme dishabille. "Your Grace . . . !"

Kerne, however, had turned, and, letting himself out the way they had entered, was already well on his way down the stairs, leaving Eudora staring in dazed perplexity after him.

Chapter 4

"I admit I was wrong about the Earl of Bremington, Eudora," declared Eleanor, Lady Brockhurst, accepting a dish of tea from her cousin. "I knew, of course, that he once had a certain reputation for sowing wild oats, but that was years ago. For heaven's sake, he is all of forty now. I thought, since he is anxious to set up his nursery, he must surely have got some sense in his head."

"To say he has more hair than wit would seem particularly apropos," Eudora responded dryly, "since he is nearly devoid of the former. Not that I have any objections to bald men," she added reflectively. "I have always thought Papa was exceptionally handsome with his unadorned pate, and he, at least, never tried to hide it beneath a badly done wig. Bremington, however, displays all the appeal of a rampaging bull. I am quite certain he would have stopped at nothing to compromise me into marrying him. Marigale Little had hardly retired to her room to freshen up after our journey, than the earl lured me downstairs and practically jumped me in the foyer. And then, when I managed to get away from him, he grabbed me outside the door to my room."

"Dear me, how was I to know?" said Eleanor on a plaintive note, her green eyes rueful. "I was only thinking of you, dearest cousin. You know I should never wish anything ill to befall you."

"Of course you would not," Eudora readily agreed. "On the other hand, if you really wished the best for me, you would give up trying to lure me into marriage. How can I convince you that I am perfectly content to remain a spinster? Or that, indeed, I should much prefer it."

"But how can you, Eudora?" Setting her cup in its saucer on her knee, Eleanor gazed earnestly across the tea table at her cousin. "You are a warm, loving, beautiful woman, who deserves better than to live alone. You should have a husband and children to fill your days."

"I already have plenty to occupy me without the added burden of a husband," Eudora did not hesitate to inform her. "Furthermore, whenever I am laboring under the urge for children to fill my days, I have only to entertain Cornelius's. Believe me, a day or two playing auntie to his five young hopefuls is more than enough to quell any yearnings for children I might have."

"Heavens, I daresay that would discourage anyone's motherly instincts," Eleanor agreed, screwing her lovely face up in a comical grimace. "On the other hand, that is not at all the same thing as having one's own, believe me, Eudora."

"No, at least I know with Cornelius's that I shall eventually be able to return them to their parents," observed Eudora, serenely taking a sip from her cup. "Has it never occurred to you, Eleanor, that there are some women who live perfectly full lives in the single state?"

"No, my dear, it has not. However, I confess that I may be prejudiced, since I have had the good fortune to be married these past six years to my dearest Teddie. He is everything that I should ever wish in a husband, and more.

All I have ever wanted for you is that you might enjoy the same sort of happiness that I have known.''

"When I meet a man like Teddie, you may be sure that I shall give the possibility of marriage my full consideration,'' Eudora assured her cousin. "In the meantime, I should be best pleased if you left me to determine my own life. No more matchmaking ploys, Eleanor, I beg you.''

"Very well, Eudora, if that is what you truly want,'' Eleanor said, crossing her fingers beneath the folds of her dress. "I give up. I shall not even insist you come with me to the ball Lady Everston is giving for her granddaughter's coming-out, though it promises to be the event of the Season. I have it from a reliable source that the Duke of Kerne has promised to be in attendance. Can you imagine that? But then, of course, Lady Everston is, after all, his godmama and probably the only female His Grace does not hold in contempt. Still, the Devil Incarnate at a debutante ball! I daresay it boggles the mind.''

"Yes, I suppose it does,'' admitted Eudora with a somewhat distracted air. Only hearing the duke's name was enough to throw her into a state of confusion. And in truth, His Grace had been a great deal on her mind since her single aborted attempt to enlist his aid in ruining her for her own sake. Strange that the one man noted for his utter lack of scruples should have refused to perform this one small favor for her, she reflected. But then, he *had* declared that the next time she placed herself in such a position she would not escape so easily. No doubt, more a man of honor than he would have anyone believe, he simply required additional proof that she was perfectly serious in her intent to see herself permanently removed from the lists of marriageable females. In which case, her obvious next step in her campaign was to arrange another opportunity to place herself in his power.

Inexplicably, her heartbeat accelerated at the mere thought of such a prospect. Indeed, she was peculiarly aware of a distinct light-headedness, which she attributed to her having skipped breakfast in favor of perusing an account of Caroline Lucretia Herschel's discovery of seven comets, not to mention several nebulae and stars, which were recorded in her famous brother's catalogues.

"You cannot know how glad I am to hear you say so, Eleanor," said Eudora, nonchalantly taking a bite of a ginger cookie. "And because you do not intend to insist or cajole me into attending Lady Everston's ball, I shall gladly go with you."

"You will?" said Eleanor blankly.

"But of course I shall." Irresistibly, Eudora laughed. "You cannot think I should wish to miss the event of the Season, can you?"

It was evident long before Eudora stepped down from the carriage that Lady Everston's ball was a shocking squeeze. The long line of conveyances still waiting a turn to draw up to the house was sufficient evidence that everyone who was anyone would be there tonight.

In spite of her instinctively reclusive nature, Eudora was well acquainted among the *ton*. As the Duke of Umberly's niece, it could hardly have been otherwise. In her first Season, she had enjoyed a considerable success. By, this, her fifth Season, having turned down any number of proposals from eligible partis, she was accounted a Diamond of the First Water, an Original, and an Avowed Spinster, who seldom deigned to make an appearance at the seasonal whirl of social events. Had it not been for her cousin Eleanor's manipulations, it was probable that she would have faded into obscurity. As it was, she was greeted by any number of old acquaintances, who evinced a sincere pleasure in her company.

Nor was she allowed to become a wallflower ensconced along the sidelines. Having established a small, but loyal, following of friends among the older set of Fashionables, she was kept dancing as much as she liked and otherwise

entertained with a lively discussion of her favorite topic—
astronomical observations.

It was perhaps due to her unusual obsession that she
had attracted the notice of the more jaded members of
her set. Lord Danville, a man more than twice her age
who was noteworthy for having outlived three wives, not
to mention numerous opponents on the field of honor, was
only one of several. Taking Mr. Woodrow's seat, vacated
for the purpose of fetching Eudora a glass of punch, his
lordship engaged to inquire into her latest discoveries
among the heavenly bodies.

"Strange that you should have asked," replied Eudora,
her lovely face lighting up, even as Danville had known
that it would. "As it happens, I have only just had the
immense satisfaction of proving some calculations I made
a little over three years ago were indisputably accurate."

"That must have been exceedingly gratifying," observed
Danville, propping his chin on one hand, his elbow resting
on the arm of his chair as he observed the heavenly lights
in Miss Precious's intriguingly blue-violet eyes.

"Indeed, sir, it was," agreed Eudora, oblivious to the
stir in the crowd occasioned by the arrival of a tall, elegantly
clad figure descending the staircase into the ballroom. "It
has enabled me to predict the arrival of a particular comet
every 3.3 years. Furthermore, by tabulating its appearances
backwards in time, I should now be able to identify it in
numerous historical references. It would be rather like
tracing the life of a very dear, very old friend through the
ages."

"Fascinating," remarked Danville, a deal more en-
thralled by the play of emotion in the young beauty's ani-
mated visage. "Perhaps you would care to show me this
comet of yours. I daresay the terrace would offer ideal
conditions for a viewing."

Eudora, ever disposed to gaze at the stars, was not loath
to comply. "A capital idea, my lord," she agreed, smiling
as she rose with alacrity to her feet. Intent on looking upon

her prized comet, she failed to note a pair of exceedingly hard eyes, like blue glints of steel between slitted eyelids, follow her progress with Lord Danville through the crowd and out the French doors to the terrace.

It was a singularly fine, cloudless evening with the added bonus of a new moon to lend the stars an unusual clarity and brilliance. Eudora, leaning against the terrace wall, pointed to the comet, a small silver blaze against an indigo backdrop.

"There, my lord," she said, feeling the familiar surge of excitement. "Is it not a spectacular sight?"

"I daresay I have never seen anything *more* spectacular," declared Danville, gazing down at Eudora's rapt features. "It fairly takes my breath away."

Startled by his profuse response, Eudora glanced suspiciously up into Danville's lean, still-handsome countenance. "I was referring to the comet, my lord," she pointed out dryly.

"And I was referring to something lovelier by far, my dear. A pity I am not ten years younger. The sight of you in the starlight is enough to conjure up notions of conjugal bliss. I don't suppose you would consider marrying a widower with three grown children older than you."

"If it were you, my lord, I should be sorely tempted," Eudora retorted, laughing. "I daresay you would be the ideal sort of husband for me—not so young as to be wishing to rule my life for me and not so old that you are not terribly attractive."

A smile of wry amusement played about the stern lips. "But not tempting enough for you to marry me, is that it?"

"I'm afraid not, my lord," Eudora answered with characteristic frankness. "I should sooner be the mistress of a man I did not love than his wife. At least, then, when the feelings are gone, we should be free to go our separate ways."

"An enchanting notion, Miss Precious," observed a new,

masculine voice from behind the couple on the terrace, "but hardly practical, would you say, Danville?"

Eudora, stifling a gasp of surprise at that soft, thrilling drawl, came around to behold the Duke of Kerne, a broad shoulder propped negligently against a fluted column and his eyes glittering coldly in the spill of light from the ballroom.

"But of course it is practical, Your Grace," Eudora declared, quelling the absurd leap of her pulse. "Being logical-minded, I am always eminently practical in my thinking. What you mean to say is that it is not at all *comme il faut.*"

"That, too," agreed the duke smoothly, his gaze peculiarly fixed on Danville, who returned his look with a glint of amusement.

"It was all purely hypothetical, Your Grace, assure you," Danville drawled in such a manner as to leave little doubt he found the Devil Incarnate's interest in Miss Precious and her original thought processes more than a little provocative.

The devil, cursed the duke silently to himself. He had hardly expected, upon arriving at Lady Everston's ball, to see the meddlesome Miss Precious, looking even more beautiful than he remembered her, in a shimmering gown the blue-violet of her eyes, the same eyes that had haunted him the past several days, invading his dreams and serving as a constant reminder of the sudden and unexpected birth of hitherto unsuspected chivalrous instincts in one who had never before felt the smallest compunction in using a woman for his own purposes.

The devil take her. Upon espying the little baggage in what gave every appearance of an intimate conversation with Danville, he had suffered a sharp, unfamiliar stab of something suspiciously resembling jealousy. That, however, had been nothing compared to the sudden hard clamp on his vitals as he beheld the young beauty rise and slip out onto the terrace in Danville's company.

His first thought, that Miss Precious was indeed intent on getting herself ruined, so intent, in fact, that, having failed to elicit his own participation, she had turned to Danville to ask his services on behalf of her "noble" venture, was sufficient to narrow his lips to a thin, hard line.

Danville! Egad! Besides being more than twice her age, the nobleman was a notorious libertine, a man noted for his dissolute lifestyle, his gambling, and his propensity for dueling. If she had chosen Danville to breach the Bastion of Virginity, she would soon discover she had found a veritable prince of nobility. Eudora Precious would be deflowered and defamed before the bloody night was over!

He was to speculate later that he must have suffered a momentary aberration or taken leave of his senses. Certainly, he could not recall another time in which he had exerted himself in the defence of a woman's Inviolable Virtue. Stepping out on to the terrace, he had been just in time not only to see Miss Precious gazing up into her companion's dissolute countenance with an aspect of angelic innocence, but to overhear her refuse an offer of marriage in favor of becoming Danville's mistress!

"As it happens, my lord," returned the duke with a chilling velvet-edged softness, "I take a particular interest in Miss Precious, who is an old friend of mine. Hypothetically speaking, you might say I should take exception if anyone were to misinterpret her unique manner of thinking."

"Believe it or not, Your Grace, so should I," remarked Danville, his smile decidedly wry. "Miss Precious, a pleasure as always. Your Grace," he murmured, and, inclining his head, turned and left them.

"Well," declared Eudora profoundly, upon finding herself suddenly alone with the Duke of Kerne. "What in heaven's name was *that* all about? No doubt you will pardon my confusion, Your Grace, but I was not aware that you had the smallest interest in me, let alone that we were old friends. Furthermore, I believe I stated my convictions with perfect clarity. I cannot think there was any room for misinterpretation."

"Oh, with perfect clarity, Miss Precious," Kerne agreed with a singular lack of humor. "You may be certain Danville understood precisely what you were saying. And you are quite right. Whatever ridiculous thing you might choose to do or say next is of no concern to me. Now that we understand one another, I suggest we return to the ballroom where you will favor me with the dance now in progress, after which, I shall leave you to your friends."

"How very proper of you, Your Grace," observed the redoubtable Miss Precious, regarding him with a look from her lovely eyes that left him little doubt she was rapidly reassessing her opinion of him.

"Quite so, Miss Precious. It would seem you have the unhappy knack of bringing out the best in me. Another hour in your company, and I should no doubt be a reformed character."

"Yes, and it is most disagreeable of you, too," Eudora conceded testily. "I chose you precisely because you are the Devil Incarnate. I must say, Your Grace, you have failed thus far to live up to your reputation."

His reputation! Egad, she had not the least notion to what extent she had deterred him from his normal course, he reflected, feeling the effect of her influence over him in the sudden stir of his loins. *Damn* the chit! He had met many women who readily aroused his primitive male passions, but never before one who resurrected what he had considered his long-dead honorable instincts, a phenomenon, to which, if Kerne had read him correctly, Danville had also found himself prey. The duke doubted there was any other woman who, under similar circumstances, would have walked away from both Danville and the Devil Incarnate with her virtue intact.

"No doubt I am sorry to disappoint you," he murmured, his smile mirthless. "On the other hand, it is my custom never to be agreeable to anyone. Now, if you are ready . . . ?"

Holding out his arm to her, he waited.

"Oh, very well," Eudora said, grudgingly placing her gloved hand on his. "Though I must say it is most ungenerous of you. I suppose you realize that by singling me out to dance with you, you are only adding to my problem. Instead of being ruined, I shall become an overnight success. I daresay I shall be inundated with invitations and moonstricken swains eager to fling themselves at my feet."

"A hideous prospect," observed the duke dryly, leading her into the ballroom and on to the dance floor.

"It is, in fact, the shabbiest thing," agreed Eudora, as he swung her into the gliding steps of the waltz already in progress. "You might at least hold me indecently close, Your Grace," she suggested, gazing up at him in what she no doubt hoped would appear provocative to the roomful of gawking onlookers. "If you will not ruin me in reality, you might at least give the impression that we have been intimately acquainted. It is, after all, the truth. Certainly, no one else has ever gained a more personal knowledge of my proclivity for powerful emotions."

Eudora, who had been wondering if he had forgotten that particular aspect of their last meeting, was startled to see a faint tinge of color touch his chiseled features.

"You will receive a deal more than that, Miss Precious," he warned in steely accents, "if ever you tempt me again. I am not noted for my forbearance in such matters."

"But it is not your forbearance that I wish, Your Grace," Eudora did not hesitate to remind him. "I thought I made that much at least quite clear to you."

"And I, Miss Precious, am not given to being manipulated by women." He was, in fact, demmed if he would oblige her. He had been seduced once by a woman with a cold, calculated purpose. He had prided himself on the fact that he had never, since that one youthful indiscretion, given in to a female's personal agenda. He was bloody well demmed if he would break that rule now.

Unfortunately, he could not but note that the maddening Miss Precious fitted his arms to perfection or that, light on her feet and naturally graceful, she seemed an ethereal creature, not quite of this world, who was capable of making him feel as if he were floating on air.

He was aware of an unwonted regret when the music stopped and he was forced to remove his arm from about her slender waist, a realization that did nothing to improve his already sorely tried temper.

Escorting Miss Precious to her seat near her cousin, he bowed over Eudora's hand, then, vowing to make certain he never laid eyes on the Angel of Seduction again, he left her to stare after him, a dreamy, rather dazed, look on her angelic features.

Chapter 5

"You may tell Lord Chelsea I am not at home to callers," Eudora declared irritably to her butler. "Tell them *all* I have departed for the Orient or some other equally inaccessible foreign place and expect never to return. Or tell them I expired, I care not, so long as I am left alone."

"Very well, miss," said the servant, his wooden expression revealing nothing of his thoughts at facing a withdrawing room filled with any number of gentlemen intent on paying their addresses to Miss Eudora Precious. "And the marquess, your cousin, miss?"

"You mean Lansbury?" exclaimed his mistress, considerably brightening. "Felix is here?"

"I left his lordship in the solarium sampling one of Mrs. Cranston's quince pies. Did you wish me to inform him you are not home to callers?"

"Heavens, no, Quimby," exclaimed Eudora, flinging aside the computations upon which she had been trying unsuccessfully to concentrate. "Tell his lordship I shall be down directly."

"As you wish, Miss Eudora," intoned Quimby, bowing and withdrawing.

Eudora, attired in a morning dress of sprig muslin, paused only long enough to pat her short blond curls in place before slipping out the door of her study. Desirous of avoiding a chance encounter with her bevy of new admirers, she took the servants' stairs down to the ground floor and proceeded by the back way to the solarium, where a slender youth in rider's garb stood, one long leg draped over the edge of a table as he consumed with apparent enjoyment what appeared to be one of Mrs. Cranston's famous quince pies.

"Felix," she exclaimed with unadulterated pleasure. "How *good* to see you. I had no idea you were in Town."

"I'm not," replied Felix around a hefty mouthful of sweetened pears, golden brown crust, and cinnamon. Chewing, then swallowing, he expanded, "At least not officially. So far as Papa and Mama are concerned, I am in Oxford with my tutor, brushing up on my Aristotle. You won't tell them any differently, will you, Dorie?"

"Felix, you have been sent down. Again!" declared Eudora, eyeing with humorous censure the handsome youth, his blond, curly locks, falling in charming disarray over the smooth forehead above remarkably blue eyes. "What in the world did you do this time?"

"Nothing much, assure you, Coz," replied the young rapscallion, grinning with a lopsided boyish charm. "Only introduced a goat into the headmaster's bedchamber. Was not anything he did not deserve, the old crotchet. Besides, I needed a holiday away from school. Beastly place, school. Decided it was time I paid a visit to my favorite cousin. How are the stars, Dorie? Find any new ones lately?"

"I haven't time to study the stars these days," Eudora said with a dour expression. "I am much too busy staving off the flood of admirers who have been swarming at my door the past several days. And all because the Duke of Kerne decided to dance with me at Lady Everston's ball.

I swear I have not had a moment of peace since that dreadful night.''

"I say, Dorie. The Duke of Kerne?" queried Felix, finishing off the last morsel of pie and licking his fingers. "Why the deuce should the Devil Incarnate wish suddenly to make *you* a success? Beg your pardon, old girl, but you are hardly in his usual style of females."

"As it happens, he has made it clear I am not at all in his style of females," Eudora asserted with a wry grimace. "I am, in fact, in danger of making a reformed character of him, which is why he has determined never again to come into my unsavory sphere of influence. How detestable it is! Just when I had come to a solution to Eleanor's matchmaking manipulations, the man I chose to be the instrument of my salvation suddenly develops a conscience."

"Demmed inconsiderate of him," replied Felix, who had made little sense of his cousin's rather wild ramblings, but who knew Eudora well enough to realize it all made perfect sense to her. "Clearly grounds for a duel. Only give me the word, Dorie, and I shall call him out."

"I wish you would not be absurd, Felix," Eudora retorted. "Even if there were any danger His Grace would accept the challenge of a seventeen-year-old—and there *is* not—I wish you to do no such thing. I should hope you are far too intelligent to ever engage in anything so patently foolish as a meeting at dawn."

"Nothing foolish about it, Dorie. You only say that because you're a girl. Dueling is a man's business. Got nothing to do with female sensibilities. Has to do with honor and valor on the field of battle, all that sort of thing."

"I fail to see the least thing honorable or valorous in facing off at dawn with drawn pistols. It is, in fact, a wholly irrational act, and the only reason it is a masculine one is because women are far too sensible to engage in it. No, I'm afraid there is nothing to be done short of barricad-

ing myself in the house until all of this has died down.
Unless . . .''

Eudora went suddenly quite still, a peculiar, arrested
look on her face, as though she had just been struck by
divine inspiration. "Perhaps there *is* something you can
do for me," she said, turning to gaze conspiratorially at
her young cousin. "You did say you needed a holiday. How
would you like to take a drive to Claverly? The woods are
always delightful this time of year."

The Duke of Kerne, stepping down from his carriage
and entering his private club, was made instantly aware
that something was afoot. Not only did a silence fall over
the entire company at his entrance, followed by a sudden
drone of conversation, but he was for a brief moment the
cynosure of attention before all eyes turned away with
studied *sang-froid.*

All eyes, that was, save for those of Lord Danville, who
regarded the duke with sardonic interest. Unaccountably,
Kerne experienced an uncanny sense of foreboding.

"Danville," Kerne murmured, inclining his head in recognition as he made to stroll past the nobleman.

"Ah, Kerne," remarked Lord Danville, casually retriev-
ing an exquisite enameled snuff box from his coat pocket.
Flipping open the lid with his thumb, he extracted a pinch
of his favorite mixture and inhaled it before putting the
box away again. "I hardly expected to see you here today,
Your Grace."

"Did you not?" A single arrogant eyebrow arched toward
the duke's hairline. "I fail to see why today should be
different from any other."

"Indeed? But then, I feel sure I did not misunderstand
you. You did say, did you not, that you entertained a particular interest in a certain young beauty? Yes, I am sure you
did, in spite of my lamentably poor memory. In which case,
one can only presume that you have not heard the news."

"Since I have only just left my house to come directly to the club, you may be sure of it," returned Kerne, keenly aware that Danville was enjoying himself at his expense. "Has something happened to the lady in question?"

"Perhaps it is nothing to concern you. However, it has been reported by Lord Chelsea, and attested to by a handful of others who called at the lady's home this morning, that she was seen apparently being bundled in no little hurry into a coach by a gentleman who was later identified as the Marquess of Lansbury."

Kerne felt a cold fist close on his vitals, a circumstance which he did not betray by even so much as the blink of an eyelash. "Then I daresay Chelsea was mistaken in thinking the lady was in peril," he observed dispassionately. "Surely he must be as aware as I that the Marquess of Lansbury is her cousin."

"You are right, of course," agreed Danville. "And so I reassured Chelsea. Still, I cannot but wonder if Miss Precious was entirely amenable to a family reunion at this time. Rumor has it that her eldest brother favors a match with Lansbury in spite of the age difference. A matter of keeping the ducal fortune intact, I believe. Still," Danville shrugged, "you are undoubtedly in the right of it. It is clearly a family matter and hardly of any concern to an outsider. In which case I shall just wish you a good day, Your Grace."

Kerne, watching Danville saunter away, could not but wonder why he should find the nobleman's shrug of dismissal somehow less than comforting. It was clearly none of Kerne's business if Miss Precious had departed from her home in a coach with her cousin. If it was indeed an elopement as everyone appeared to believe, then at least the troublesome Miss Precious would be finally settled and beyond the need for any of her hare-brained schemes to remove herself from the lists of marriageable females. He should be relieved to be quit of the entire matter.

That, perversely, he felt no satisfaction at this conclusion,

indeed, that he recalled with vivid clarity Eudora's avowal
that he had not the least notion to what lengths her relatives would go to see her married, served to conjure up
disquieting images of the Bastion of Virginity in the power
of soulless tyrants.

Who the devil *was* this Marquess of Lansbury? he wondered, unaware that the sudden steely glint in his eyes
occasioned Mr. Finchley of the Essex Finchleys at whom
it seemed to be directed to go a sickly shade of grey. If
the bloody marquess was of an age to be married, then
why had he never been presented in Town? Perhaps there
were reasons why Eudora had been willing to go to extreme
measures to avoid an alliance with the Duke of Umberly's
heir apparent, speculated the Devil Incarnate, his lips thinning to a grim line. It was not unheard of to have half-
wits, degenerates or even the criminally insane in line to
inherit among the noble houses. Normally they would be
kept under wraps, but occasionally, especially in instances
when the heir was an only son, a marriage to insure the
continuation of the line might be arranged.

An image of Eudora, beautiful, forthright and angelically
innocent, rose up to haunt Kerne. The very thought of
the singular Miss Precious forced into an unwholesome
marriage was not one he could contemplate with ease. It
was, in fact, not to be tolerated.

Spinning on his heel, the duke strode purposefully out
of his club.

Thirty minutes later, having ascertained through the
bribery of a scullery maid that the Marquess of Lansbury
had set out with Miss Precious for Umberly's hunting lodge
near Marlow, Kerne was driving his matched team of greys
at a splitting pace out of London, with Trist, his groom,
sitting wooden-faced beside him. Indeed, having calculated
that Lansbury must have at least a five-hour lead on him
was enough to inspire Kerne to what in anyone else would
have been a reckless daring. Kerne, however, had not
earned the reputation of being a top of the trees sawyer

for nothing. Driving with consummate skill, he had swiftly
left the traffic of London behind him.

"Are you quite sure Umberly has no intention of using
the lodge anytime soon?" demanded Eudora, kneeling to
light the fire already laid out in the great fireplace.

"Papa never comes down while Parliament is seated.
You know that, Dorie." Felix, rummaging through the
picnic basket Mrs. Cranston had hurriedly supplied,
helped himself to a roasted chicken leg before flopping
down on the velvet-covered sofa ranged before the fireplace. "Mama would not hear of it. She is far too jealous
of her position as London's leading hostess ever to miss a
Season in London."

"Yes, but Cornelius does not usually make it a habit to
descend on Hardwicke Court with his five offspring while
the duke is in residence," Eudora pointed out. "If I were
Umberly, I should wish to find a secure haven for escape."

"You *did* wish for a secure haven of escape," Felix did
not hesitate to remind her, as he stretched his long legs
out before him. "And now you have found one. I daresay
no one will bother you here. Devilishly isolated, Claverly,"
Felix added with a shudder. "Might as well have entered
a nunnery. Are you certain you don't want me to stay on
with you? Now that we're here, I'm not in the least sure I
should leave you to fend for yourself."

"It is far too late for second thoughts, Felix," Eudora
demurred, thinking the last thing she could wish was to
have her seventeen-year-old cousin around to cut up her
peace and distract her from her work. She had not gone
to all the trouble to elude her plethora of suitors in order
to be saddled with someone whom she must look after
and entertain. "I suggest it is time you took the coach and
started back to London. You are perfectly welcome to make
my house your home until you have figured out how you
are going to face Umberly with your latest peccadillo."

"You do not really expect me to leave you here without some sort of companion, Dorie?" demanded Felix, tossing the chicken bone into the fireplace. "Not the thing, you know. Bad *ton* and all that sort of thing."

"I am a woman of three and twenty, Felix, which is far beyond the age of requiring a chaperone. You, on the other hand, are an adolescent fugitive from justice. I suggest if you do not want me to turn you over to Umberly, you do precisely as we originally planned."

"Aw, Dorie," grimaced Felix, crestfallen. "Turn me over to Umberly? Say you didn't mean it. You never used to be mean-spirited."

"Nor am I being so now, Felix. I am simply reminding you of our agreement. At least trust me to know what I am doing. Now, off with you. I have a deal of work to do."

Unfolding his lanky length from the sofa, Felix eyed his cousin doubtfully. "All right, I'm going, but I cannot help worrying about you, Dorie. What if someone like the Devil Incarnate happened on to you all alone here, with no one to protect you? I daresay he would not hesitate to take advantage of his opportunity. It would be your ruination, and it would be all my fault for abandoning you to your fate."

"Now you are being absurd," objected Eudora, dismayed to feel a hot rush of blood to her cheeks at such a prospect. "Kerne is the last person I should expect to show up on my doorstep, and if he did, you may be sure he would behave like a perfect gentleman. I am in no danger from the Devil Incarnate, or anyone else, for that matter."

It was with a deal of urging that Eudora was finally able to send Felix on his way with the promise that he would dispatch the coach for her in three days. Breathing a sigh of relief, Eudora returned to the lodge and laid out her charts and papers. Then, taking up her traveling telescope, she climbed to the attic with the intention of devising an observation deck on the roof before nightfall.

* * *

The fact that he had driven the distance to Marlow in
record time did little to alleviate the pressure in Kerne's
breast, as he pulled up before the posting inn on the
outskirts of the town. Having spent the entire journey
contemplating Eudora in the unsavory hands of relatives
who would stop at nothing to achieve their ends, he presented a grim aspect to the hostlers who scrambled to tend
his cattle.

"Walk 'em," he ordered curtly, "and see that they are
properly fed and bedded down. There's a shilling in it for
each of you if you have a new team in the traces in less
than ten minutes. And another to the lad who can tell me
the swiftest way to Umberly's hunting lodge."

"I can tell yer, gov," piped up a grinning lad.

Less than ten minutes later, having left Trist with a purse
and instructions to return the team home by easy stages
on the morrow, Kerne swept out of the courtyard into the
deepening dusk.

The Duke of Umberly's hunting lodge, nestled in a clear-
ing deep in the Quarry Woods, might, at another time,
have impressed Kerne as a lovely, secluded spot ideal for
a weekend escape from London. Certainly, the two-story
house with its dormered attic windows and its walls covered
with clematis offered a tranquil setting amidst beech and
silver birch trees, abounding, he did not doubt, with pheas-
ant and deer. In his present frame of mind, however, it
loomed not so much as a picturesque haven, but as a
cursedly isolated place that offered an ideal setting for
laying siege to the Bastion of Innocence.

Grimly leaping down from the seat of his curricle, the
duke secured the horses. Then, steeling himself for the
confrontation that lay ahead, he strode boldly for the door.

Having spent the past two and a half hours envisioning
Eudora being browbeaten and coerced by her scheming
relatives, Kerne was prepared to be met with hostility and

certainly a cold incredulity at his temerity in meddling in something that was clearly none of his affair. What he did not expect, upon slamming the knocker three times in succession with enough force to set the windows rattling, was to have the silence suddenly and chillingly shattered by a high-pitched, bloodcurdling scream.

Feeling the hairs rise at the nape of his neck, not to mention a sharp stab of horror, like a knife thrust to his heart, Kerne uttered a blistering oath. Good God, *Eudora!* he thought.

The next instant he had thrust open the door and bounded across the threshold into the roomy, well-apportioned hall, made cheerful with a lighted brass chandelier, high-beamed ceiling and wide oaken stairway. A door left open offered a glimpse of an even cozier sitting room warmed by a crackling fire in the stone fireplace. What there was not, however, was any sign of Eudora or her apparently murderous relatives.

Baffled, his heart pounding in the brooding quiet, Kerne leaped for the staircase.

The cry came as his foot found the first step—a high, piercing cry, accompanied by a muffled scrape and thump. Then, abruptly, nothing. Kerne froze in the crushing silence.

The devil, he thought. It had seemed to come from somewhere outside the house.

Turning, he snatched up a lighted lamp and lunged out into the moon-clouded dark.

"*Eudora! Eudora!* For God's sake, Eudora, *answer me!* Where the devil are you?"

"Good God, Kerne," came back to him in unmistakable tones of horror. "Is that *you?*"

"Of course it is. Who else should it be, you absurd child?" Lifting the lamp high, he searched the darkness around him.

"My God, it *is* you. The last man in the world I should have wished to find me like this," seemed to waft down to him out of the treetops. "Pray go away at once, Your Grace. I should rather die than have you see me in my present state."

Die? Good God, she *was* in a vulnerable case, thought Kerne, feeling a cold rage start in the pit of his stomach. His fearless angel. What the devil had they done to her? "Nonsense," he called out, striving for a bracing tone. "I've come to take you home, Eudora."

"I've no wish to go home. Pray go away. At once, Your Grace. I swear I shall never forgive you if you do not."

"Enough, Eudora. Now you *are* being absurd. You have nothing to fear from me, child. Only tell me where you are."

The duke's fist clenched tight in the unnerving stretch of answering silence.

Then, at last, on a long sigh of resignation, "Oh, very well. Up here, Your Grace. Directly over your head. I daresay if you climb up the trellis, you can reach me."

It was only then, as Kerne peered directly overhead and the moon seemed to drift out from behind a concealing cloud, that he saw her—Eudora, a pale, gleaming figure, snatched nearly bare to the chest and dangling ignominiously by the hem of her skirt from the overhang of the roof.

"Good God," rasped the duke aghast, and nearly dropped the lamp.

Chapter 6

"This is all your fault," Eudora declared testily, as Kerne, stern-faced, carried her into the sitting room and, laying her down on the sofa, crossed to a carved oak wine cabinet amply supplied with potable wines. "If you had not danced with me at Lady Everston's ball, I should not have been driven half to distraction by a steady stream of gentlemen callers. In which case, I should not have had the least need to seek a remote haven where no one could find me. I should not, then, have been startled out of my wits by your unexpected assault on my door, causing me to precipitously lose my balance. I should not have lost my footing and slid down the slope of the roof or caught my dress on the broken edge of the gutter to be caught, dangling in what can only be described as a most unseemly manner. I should be at home in my cupola, viewing the stars and making my computations. What in heaven's name possessed you, Your Grace, to follow me to Claverly?"

Kerne, who had yet to say a word since his Herculean efforts to remove Miss Precious from her perilous plight, grimly picked up a decanter of Umberly's excellent brandy and two glasses before turning and crossing the room to face his accuser.

"Undoubtedly, like you, I was compelled to it by a perversity of fate," he offered dryly, "the sole purpose for which was to ensure I should be here in the nick of time to rescue you." Sloshing brandy into a glass, he placed it in Eudora's hand. "Here, drink this," he ordered, before pouring a second libation for himself.

"But that is absurd," Eudora protested, ignoring the brandy. "You could not possibly have known I was going to slip on the roof. Indeed, it would never have happened if you had not been here to startle me."

"No doubt," submitted the duke humorlessly and, forgoing his usual custom of examining the wine's bouquet and texture before imbibing, tossed the brandy off in a single, much-needed swallow. Promptly he refilled the glass. "But then, therein lies the irony," he commented in acerbic tones, the image of Eudora, dangling two stories above his head, yet burned into his consciousness. "As it happens, I arrived, expecting to find you in the clutches of your heartless relatives intent on forcing you into marriage with the Marquess of Lansbury, your criminally insane cousin. Good God, what a jest." Mirthlessly, he laughed; then, throwing back his head, downed the potent contents of the glass. "Where, by the way, is the villain?"

"Where is who?" echoed Eudora, apparently taken aback at this new turn of events. "Surely you cannot mean my Cousin Felix?"

"I daresay you would know your cousin better than I," replied Kerne caustically. "It was you who informed me your brother Cornelius favored the match."

"But that is absurd," Eudora declared, clearly suspecting the duke of having taken leave of his senses. "Felix is only a boy, and he is as sane as you or I. Furthermore, there has never been any question of my marrying him. It was just some silly thing Cornelius thought up. No one ever took it seriously."

"The Earl of Chelsea took it seriously. And he was hardly the only one. You may be sure your supposed abduction by Lansbury is being discussed in every salon in London by now."

"But that is absurd, there was never any abduction," exclaimed Eudora, envisioning the probable reaction to the news among her numerous relatives. "Felix only came along to make sure I should arrive safely. We took every precaution to avoid being seen in order to elude my suitors. I sent him home hours ago."

"Your precautions are no doubt what lent your actions an air of suspicion. Congratulations, Miss Precious," Kerne said, lifting the glass to her, "you have finally managed to cast doubt on your Virtue Inviolable. I daresay you will have little choice, now, but to marry your cousin."

"I shall do no such thing," declared Eudora, inexplicably hurt by the duke's callous indifference. "It is all a tempest in a teapot. And what did you think to accomplish by riding *ventre à terre* in pursuit of me, Your Grace? Surely you did not think to save my good name, when I have repeatedly told you I most adamantly wish to be rid of it?"

"Whatever I thought, it can hardly signify now," countered the duke, who had not failed to note Eudora's sudden pallor. "Drink your brandy, Miss Precious," he commanded in tones that brooked no argument. Then, "The devil," he muttered, on closer inspection. "You are trembling like a leaf." Snatching up a decorative shawl draped over the back of an overstuffed wing chair, he proceeded to spread it over Eudora. "I daresay the blame may be laid at my doorstep that you were on that cursed roof. I should nevertheless be interested to know what the devil you were doing up there after nightfall."

"I was observing the stars, Your Grace," Eudora answered crossly. "Pray tell what else should I be doing? And you still have not answered my question."

"Nor have you done as I ordered," he pointed out. Dropping to one knee beside the sofa, he took the glass

from her and held it to her lips so that Eudora had little
choice but to swallow a hefty portion of the vile-tasting
stuff. "Yes, that is more like," the duke grimly approved,
noting the returning flush of color in Eudora's cheeks.
His eyebrows fairly snapped together at the shimmer of
tears in her eyes. "Absurd child, what is it? Tell me, are
you hurt somewhere?"

"But of course I am hurt," Eudora retorted, mortified
at the wild leap of her pulse at his nearness, not to mention
the disconcerting urge to fling her arms around him. It
really was not in the least fair that he should have this
unsettling power over her, when to all appearances, he
himself was wholly impervious to her greatly alleged
charms. "I am bruised and battered, and I daresay my
pride has suffered a humiliating blow from which it will
never recover. You see before you a shattered woman."

"I see a woman who should know better than to set
up an observatory on a pitched roof," Kerne countered
harshly. His lip curled sardonically as Eudora stuck her
tongue out at him. "Quite so, Miss Precious," he commented dryly. "And so very ladylike. Turn over."

"I will not, Your Grace," Eudora answered, eyeing him
doubtfully over the shawl clutched to her chin. "As it
happens, I am perfectly content as I am."

"And I intend to examine you, Miss Precious, to make
sure you have sustained no serious injury. Now, do as I
say."

Eudora, who had for some time been ruefully aware of
a searing pain in her backside, decided after a single, long
assessing glance at His Grace that protest was very likely
fruitless. The Devil Incarnate was perfectly capable of picking her up and flipping her over by brute force, if need
be, to have his way.

"Oh, very well, if you must," Eudora said grudgingly.
Tossing aside the decorative shawl, she gingerly maneu-
vered herself onto her stomach. "I daresay there is nothing
you have not already seen at any rate," she concluded

fatalistically, propping her chin on the backs of her folded
hands and steeling herself for what was coming next.

"Very sensible of you, Miss Precious," observed His
Grace with sardonic appreciation of her practical outlook.
"Try and think of me as your doctor, if that will help."

"I shall try, Your Grace," Eudora promised heroically,
ironically aware that Dr. Liscombe, her family physician,
had never caused her to feel so much as a blush during
his examinations, let alone ignited a slow-burning fire in
her veins that threatened a loss of composure. "I do not,
however, hold out much hope of success. I was never one
to lend myself to playing doctor behind the stables."

"No, I daresay you were far too preoccupied with heavenly pursuits," the duke surmised, carefully undoing the
buttons at the back of her ruined blue serge gown. "I'm
afraid your dress is beyond salvation. I trust you have
brought a change with you."

"As difficult as it may be for you to believe, Your Grace,
I am generally considered a female of uncommon good
sense," Eudora retorted, acutely aware of his fingers, moving, feather-light, down her back, creating a ripple of pleasure all the way to her toes. "Of course I brought a change
of dress." To fortify her courage, she reached for the glass
of brandy he had poured for her.

"I should believe 'uncommon,' at any rate," professed
the duke, grasping both sides of the bodice and ripping
the dress from hip to hem. Nor did he stop there. Noting
a tear in her drawers, he did not hesitate to bare that part
of her anatomy as well. His lips thinned to a grim line as
he was given to see the scrape that, running over the
rounded perfection of her left buttocks, showed an angry
red against the ivory purity of her skin. "The devil," he
cursed.

"I beg your pardon?" queried Eudora, feeling, in spite
of the sudden exposure of the entirety of her backside to
the elements, peculiarly warm and perhaps a trifle light-
headed as the potent spirits explored her empty belly.

"Lie still and finish your brandy," she was ordered. "I shall have to fetch soap and warm water."

Happy to oblige, Eudora took a long pull from the glass. "I'm afraid warm water may not be so easy as you might think, Your Grace," she said, giving vent to a hiccough. "There is no one here, except for Elkins, the old caretaker, who lives in the cottage behind the lodge. I imagine he has long since gone to bed."

"I daresay I shall contrive," pronounced the duke, grimly aware that he found himself in a devil of a coil. If Miss Precious had deliberately planned to compromise herself, she had succeeded admirably. Certainly she was like no other female of refinement he had ever before encountered. He could not think of a single one who would have remotely considered setting up housekeeping in an isolated lodge for a weekend without the benefit of servants. Humorlessly, he wondered how she had thought to provide herself with the simplest of necessities, not the least of which were food and hot water for her daily ablutions.

"I never planned to stay more than a day or two," Eudora professed, correctly interpreting the scowl on his face. "Only long enough to check my computations. In case you are unaware of it, from the demise of my mother when I was nine, I was reared by my father, who was a colonel in the army. There were times when we bivouacked in the most primitive of conditions. I managed to make do." Grinning beatifically, she shoved herself up from the couch. "Come, Your Grace. Allow me to show you to the kitchens."

Eudora, feeling rather euphoric, clasped the shawl modestly to her breast with one hand and her libation of brandy in the other, and, sublimely oblivious of the delectable view she presented from behind, blithely led off in the direction of the kitchen quarters.

Kerne, who was not oblivious to it, indeed, was keenly aware of it and of the indisputable evidence that Miss

Precious was clearly three sheets to the wind, saw immediately the futility in trying to rectify the omission by any means other than removing his coat and hastily slinging it around Eudora's shoulders.

They were in luck, it soon proved. Elkins had been thoughtful enough to bank the fire in the cast-iron cookstove and to leave a pot of water warming for Miss Precious's convenience.

"How very *kind* of Elkins," exclaimed Eudora on an explosive breath. And, indeed, she was exceedingly moved, not only by the old caretaker's kind gesture, but by Kerne's heroic efforts in saving her life, a fact which she felt compelled somehow to express to him. "I believe, Your Grace," she said, weaving a trifle unsteadily on her feet, "that I have not properly thanked you yet for what you did up there." In order to clarify, she pointed an index finger ceilingward.

"Pray think nothing of it, Miss Precious," said Kerne, himself compelled to clasp her by the arms to keep her from falling.

"No, no. It might not mean a great deal to you, but it was of great significance to me." Eudora frowned as she concentrated on what she wished to say. To help her thought processes, she drained the final swig from the glass. "Perhaps I was a trifle hasty in placing all the blame on your shoulders. You did, after all, rescue me from an igno-igno-igno*mini*ous end at, I might point out, con-sid-erable risk to yourself."

"You exaggerate, Miss Precious," demurred His Grace, attempting, for safety's sake, to remove the glass from Eudora's hand. "I was never in any danger."

"Oh, but you were." Yanking the vessel of fine crystal out of his reach, Eudora swung precariously about, making a complete circle to come back face to face with the duke, who appeared, strangely, to be obscured in some sort of anomalous fog. She shook an accusatory finger at him. "Remember, I was there," she reminded him with a great show of dignity, only to have the room take that precise moment to tilt and whirl in a most disconcerting manner, a circumstance which she found absurdly funny. Giggling, she staggered forward, off-balance, and came up hard against the duke's tall frame.

"You may be sure that every detail of this day is etched permanently in my memory," replied Kerne, who having been anticipating just such an eventuality, caught her in his powerful embrace. This, he noted, she seemed to find exceedingly gratifying. Indeed, she did not even protest when he eased the glass out of her hand and set it aside.

Melting against him, Eudora instinctively clasped her arms about his neck and, allowing her head to loll back, peered with immense concentration up into that devilishly handsome countenance.

"You really are a devil, you know," she said with great seriousness after a moment, and frowned. "No matter how hard I try, I simply cannot banish you from my mind. Shabbiest thing, Your Grace. Interferes dreadfully with my work. Ever since that night in the cupola. Truth is, I've fallen terribly, hopelessly in love with you. Funny, isn't it?"

Kerne, who did not see anything the least amusing in it, indeed, who had sustained at her confession a galvanizing shock of triumph that was as startling to him as had been his angel's revelation, only just managed to keep her from slipping to the floor, as expelling a long breath, she collapsed into insensibility.

For a long moment, Kerne gazed down into her lovely countenance, a wry gleam in his eyes. Eudora loved him—terribly and hopelessly. He could not recall that anyone had ever loved him in such a way before, certainly no one among the long line of nurses and tutors who had cared for him upon the death of his mother when he was still in leading strings. And certainly none among his conquests, too numerous to count, who had all too clearly entertained a fondness for his title and his fortune, but hardly for himself. Having long since hardened his heart against the finer sensibilities, he found it exceedingly ironic that the Devil Incarnate should have won the heart of the Bastion of Innocence. He found it even more ironic that *he* loved *her*. But then, he had sensed from the very beginning that she was no common female.

She was the Angel of Seduction, who had breached the walls of the devil's defences, and now he must make certain she was not harmed by it.

Bending down, he clasped Eudora behind her knees. Then, lifting her, he turned to go up the stairs and down the corridor into the hall—to be met with the muffled rumble of horses and carriages sweeping up in front of the house. There were shouts, too, followed by the crash of the door being flung open.

"Hellsfire!" thundered in stunned accents from a tall, harassed appearing gentleman with blond, thinning hair and a squirming toddler clasped beneath either arm. "I should never have believed it, had I not seen it with my own eyes."

"Really, Cornelius, such language," objected a scandalized female with identical twin girls in tow and a third child, a boy, clinging to her skirts. "And in front of the children, too."

"I suggest, madam, that you remove your children," came the stern rejoinder from the lips of a second, middle-aged gentleman wearing the demeanor of one at the thin edge of his control, "if you do not wish their ears sullied. It was your idea to follow after your husband instead of putting up at the inn as you were instructed."

"But, Your Grace, with Nurse incapacitated with the ague, I could hardly manage all by myself. Cornelius, tell His Grace, I am generally the most conformable of wives. Besides, it was to appear a family gathering—to quell the unfortunate rumors. The duchess insisted I come for that purpose. You know she did, Your Grace."

"Pray do not remind me, madam," said the older gentleman, in an ominous tone. "The duchess, notwithstanding,

I am in no mood for feminine hysterics." Then, at last, he turned back to Kerne, who wore an expression of cynical appreciation of the peculiarity of his position. "What the devil, sir, is the meaning of this?"

"The meaning of what?" demanded Felix, inserting himself through the door, to come to a stunned halt at the scene being enacted in the hall. "Good God," he exclaimed, his jaw dropping. "Eudora and the Devil Incarnate!"

Chapter 7

Eudora, jarred into wakefulness by all the furor, stirred sluggishly in Kerne's arms and opened her eyes to behold the assemblage of astonished faces, which were regarding her with frank incredulity.

"Uncle," she exclaimed, stifling a yawn. "And Cornelius, and Hortensia and the children. Good heavens, what are you all doing here?"

"More to the point, Eudora," said the Duke of Umberly, "is what the deuce are *you* doing here in what can only be described as questionable circumstances? And you, Kerne. Where the devil do you think you are taking my niece?"

"I should have thought it was obvious, Your Grace," replied the Duke of Kerne with the sardonic arch of a single, arrogantly angled eyebrow. "I was just in the process of carrying Miss Precious up to her bed. I'm afraid I shall have to beg your indulgence for the moment. I prefer not to have the existence of my future duchess cut up just now by a lot of questions she is in no case to answer. I suggest you make yourselves comfortable inside by the fire. Have some of your excellent brandy, Umberly. This should not take too long.''

"An excellent idea," agreed Umberly, stomping without preamble off to the sitting room. "Wretched business, this, racketing about the countryside in the middle of the night. Suggest you take Hortensia and the children on to the inn, Cornelius. Daresay you'll not be needed here before morning. As for you, young man," he added sternly to Felix, "come along and we shall discuss what is to be done with you. I've a mind to send you to your uncle at the Admiralty. If that wretched school cannot make a man of you, then perhaps the King's Navy can."

"The Navy, Your Grace?" echoed Felix, clearly in alt. "I say, Papa, I should love that above all things."

"B-but, Your Grace," blustered Cornelius, "I protest. Surely you cannot expect me to abandon my sister to . . . to—"

"The Devil Incarnate?" queried his sister, finishing his sentence for him. "I do wish you would, Cornelius. Indeed, it would be devilish good of you. At any rate, I am clearly past the age of consent. There really is not a thing you can do here."

"Do not take offense, Cornelius," Kerne interjected. "Your sister is not herself at the moment, which is why I intend to see her tucked in bed for a good night's rest. Why not make it easy on yourself? It would appear you have enough on your dish at the moment. Go to the inn. You may be sure I shall join you as soon as I have settled everything here."

"Well, I suppose, if the duke and Felix are to be here to lend Eudora countenance," said Cornelius, renewing his grasp on one struggling child, then the other.

"Quite so," agreed the Devil Incarnate, proceeding up the stairs with his own Precious burden.

"But, Sylvester," protested Eudora, allowing her head to come to rest against Kerne's shoulder, conveniently placed for that very purpose, "you never told me you had a future duchess."

"I am aware of that, my angel," readily conceded the duke without pausing. "It is an omission that I was intending to correct very shortly."

"But it is a very significant omission," insisted Eudora, frowning with the effort to order her thoughts, no easy task when she was cradled in Kerne's powerful, but infinitely gentle, embrace. "You must know I should never have contrived to lure you here under false pretenses had I known you were already promised to another. It is really too bad of you, Kerne. You have placed us in a wholly untenable position."

"Pray do not concern yourself, Eudora," commanded the duke, apparently not in the least perturbed to discover he had been the object of yet another of her schemes to ruin herself. "My future bride is not in the common run of females. Having confessed to being terribly and hopelessly in love with me, I have no doubt she will eventually overcome her aversion to marrying me in order to make an honest man of me."

"You are very sure of yourself, Your Grace," Eudora retorted, eyeing him doubtfully. "I begin to suspect you have not even asked the lady for her hand yet."

"Another omission, which I shall immediately rectify." Pausing halfway up the stairs, he looked deliberately into Eudora's eyes with an intensity that quite took her breath away. "Miss Eudora Precious, would you do me the honor of becoming my wife? Before you reply, I must warn you that I am not in the least tolerant of rejection. I may be on the verge of becoming a reformed character, but I am still the Devil Incarnate. I should not hesitate to go to extreme lengths to have my way with you."

"Your previous behavior would seem to cast some doubt on that latter assertion," observed Eudora, feeling herself poised on the brink of happiness, but afraid to accept what she would seem to read in his eyes. "You have, after all, proven uncommonly reluctant to deprive me of my virtue. Why should I believe you wish to marry me, now, Your Grace, when you would have none of me when I was yours for the taking?"

"Very astute of you, my dove," applauded the Devil Incarnate, smiling approvingly down at her. "What does your superb sense of logic tell you my reason might be?"

"No doubt you will pardon me if I point out the obvious," replied Eudora, indicating the rapt audience, yet observing them from the hall below. "I do hope you are not offering out of some mistaken notion of honor, Sylvester. I refuse to be a party to trapping you into a marriage you cannot possibly want, when all I ever intended was to put an end to my cousin Eleanor's matchmaking ploys. I should never forgive myself if that proved to be the case."

"Then you may rest easy," Kerne assured her in no uncertain terms. "Your cousin's matchmaking never once entered my mind. Furthermore, if it were simply a matter of honor, you may be sure I should not hesitate to abandon you to your fate no matter how many of your relatives were gathered to protest it."

Ignoring the audible gasp from below, Kerne proceeded on to the landing.

"Then, why marriage, Your Grace, when you know perfectly well I should be content to be your mistress?" Eudora insisted, little caring that her sister-in-law appeared on the verge of succumbing to a fit of the vapors at so improper an admission from one who heretofore had been known for her Virtue Inviolable.

"Because, impossible child, I have decided in your case it is better to have the whole loaf or none at all. To have taken your virtue and let you go would seem a poor trade, would it not, when you captured me, heart and soul, that first night you descended upon me like an angel from heaven. It is time you gave the devil his due. I love you, Eudora, and I will have you as my wife, or I shall know the reason why."

"But that is easy, Your Grace," Eudora replied, reaching up to lovingly cradle the side of her dear Sylvester's face. "You must know I did not lure you here to compromise you into marrying me, even going so far as to enlist Lord Danville's part in my conspiracy. I merely hoped you would ruin me, as you promised you would if ever you had me in your power again. I am in your power, now, Sylvester. And I shall as gladly give you my virtue as my hand in marriage. After all, I have long since consigned my heart and soul to the devil."

"Then it will be the wedding first and, most assuredly, afterward your virtue," declared the duke with a smile that was distinctly satanical. "And soon, my love. No mere mortal man, not even the Devil Incarnate, can see you as it has twice been given to me to see you and be expected to leave the Bastion of Feminine Virginity unbreached for an indefinite period. I shall not wait longer than it takes to obtain a special license to make you irretrievably mine."

"Devil," said Eudora, parting her lips to him. "After all you have put me through to achieve that very thing, three days will seem like an eternity."

THE WICKED EARL

Lynn Collum

Chapter One

" 'Er's tryin' to poison me, Ma." The eight-year-old boy eyed the young miss with suspicion as he sniffed the elixir in the small flask.

"Joseph Brown, I'll box your ears if you don't take a drink of that potion this very minute. Why, Miss Markham fixed it specially to make you well and 'ere you go sayin' it's poison." Mrs. Brown shook her finger at the child whose dark eyes had grown wide at his mother's admonition.

Miss Angelica Markham's soft laughter filled the small cottage. "I promise you shall not be poisoned, Joe. I even added a bit of honey to make it go down easier."

Joe looked doubtful, but turned the flask up and took a gulp, then shuddered from head to toe. "Tastes like muck, it does—sweet muck, but muck just the same."

Angelica smiled. "Very likely, dear boy, but you'll be feeling better in no time."

Mrs. Brown planted her fists on ample hips. "And what say you to Miss Markham for comin' all the way from Edenfield Park to brin' you that cure, you grouchy whelp?"

Properly chastised the boy hung his head and meekly said, "I'm right thankful, miss."

Taking the bottle from her son as he bid the visitor goodbye, the mother placed the stopper back in place. "Miss Markham, I must tell you that all the tenants at Blackstone Abbey appreciate your lookin' after us, now that the dowager resides in Bath year round."

Angelica moved to the door of the cottage, drawing on her lace gloves. "I'm happy to help in any way I can, Mrs. Brown. Should Joe continue to feel poorly, send word and I shall try another herbal that is a bit stronger."

Joe, hearing the possibility of a new and likely viler potion, called, "I'm feelin' better already, miss."

Angelica exchanged a smile with Mrs. Brown, who opened the door for the young lady and then followed her out into the warm afternoon sunshine. Miss Markham's maid, waiting on a bench by the door, rose at the sight of her mistress. The farmer's wife glanced around for a carriage. "Why, miss, don't say you come all this way on foot. Shall I get Mr. Brown to 'itch up old Rose to the cart and take you back?"

Angelica felt her face warm. She didn't want to tell Mrs. Brown that she'd been relegated to walking now that her stepbrother had dispensed with all the horses at Edenfield save his own carriage horses. He'd deemed the others an expense he could ill afford.

"You are too kind, Mrs. Brown, but Jenny and I enjoy walking."

"Then I'll say bless you for comin', and I'll be certain to tell Lord Blackstone of your kindness to us all, should he stop by this afternoon."

Angelica's brows drew together in puzzlement. The earl being in residence at the manor in August was rare indeed. "I had not heard his lordship was returned. Is this not rather early for him?"

Mrs. Brown, misinterpreting the look as one of worry, glanced back over her shoulder, then in a lowered voice said, "Aye, 'tis early, but don't be worryin' that 'e's brought along a carriage full of fancy ladybirds like on 'is last visits. All alone the gentleman is, so you've no worry about getting 'ome without seein' such a sight. 'Tis frightful the way 'is lordship behaves, for a nicer young lad there never was."

Nodding, Angelica said her goodbyes. She and Jenny began the long trek back to Edenfield Park in silence. Her mind continued to dwell on Mrs. Brown's comments about Lord Blackstone.

For her own part, Angelica subscribed to the theory that Richard had succeeded to his title and fortune at far too young an age, making him susceptible to all the wrong elements without the guiding hand of his father. He'd become wild and reckless engaging in every kind of excess. Her late mother had declared that he would eventually outgrow such behavior, but there had been no end to the rumors making the rounds of the neighborhood.

Angelica preferred to remember Richard as the carefree young man who'd allowed a hoydenish child to tag along when he went fishing or hunting during his summers at home. She wasn't acquainted with the gentleman who'd become perhaps one of the most notorious rakes of the *ton*. If even half the rumors were true, she wasn't certain she wanted to know Richard as he'd become. Dismissing the renowned rakehell from her mind, she engaged Jenny in small talk about her family.

Nearly an hour passed before the women arrived at the door of Edenfield, hot and dusty after their long walk from the Browns's cottage in the heavy August heat. As Angelica stepped into the cool darkness of the hall, Finch, the butler, ambled forward as fast as his stooped condition would allow. The fellow should have been pensioned off years ago, but he preferred to continue working and Giles had been happy to save the expense of paying for the man's retirement.

"Ah, Miss Markham, you're here at last. Miss Parks has been askin' for you in the back parlor this past hour."

Surrendering her hat and gloves to Finch, Angelica decided to see what Harriet wished before she went up to change. "Jenny, you may have the rest of the afternoon without duties."

The young maid smiled, then curtsied and headed for the kitchen, ignoring the frown on the aged butler's face. Angelica regretted he would be left shorthanded without the servant girl. The household staff had been greatly reduced by her parsimonious stepbrother, but she knew Jenny was as tired as she from their long walk.

Angelica requested tea, then went to the woman who acted as her companion. When she entered the small parlor she discovered Miss Parks pacing the worn carpet, wringing her talonlike hands with each step.

"Good afternoon, Cousin. What has put you in the boughs?"

Harriet Parks halted and gazed at Angelica with guilty brown eyes. The spinster was a plain, frail woman, who'd unfortunately been endowed with front teeth that protruded from her thin lips. Her father had gamed away his small fortune, leaving her at the mercy of relatives. She'd resided at Edenfield Park for nearly three years under the kindness of Lady Edenfield, however, with that lady's death, her place was not so certain. Being no fool, Harriet knew that her security lay in doing whatever her young cousin Giles, Viscount Edenfield, wished. With him away, she perceived it her duty to remind everyone precisely what that gentleman's wishes were.

"At last, Angelica. Where have you been? A messenger arrived from Plymouth with a letter from your brother and you nowhere to be found," Harriet snapped waspishly. Her tone was far different from the one she used with Giles, for she considered Miss Markham in no better straits than herself.

Angelica, fatigued from the long walk, settled in a nearby

chair before she replied. "Stepbrother, dear Harriet. I
went to take some medicine to Blackstone for young Joe
Brown."

"Blackstone! Why, the viscount would be furious to hear
you walked all that way to render service to that libertine's
tenants. Thank God the earl is rarely to be found in the
district or you might have found your reputation in tat-
ters."

Angelica brushed a speck of dust from her pale blue
walking gown. She harbored a grain of satisfaction at deliv-
ering the news. "You are wrong, Harriet. The earl is
returned. I believe Richard is likely having his tea at Blackstone Abbey even as we speak."

"Tea! Ha, nothing so proper has crossed his lips since
he was a lad. And you are foolish to be calling one of such
poor reputation by his first name. You'll be having people
think you know him intimately."

"Good heavens, Harriet. Did you never know that we
grew up together? Richard and myself were often in company together when we were a good deal younger." Angelica smiled as the memory of those idyllic summer days
returned.

Harriet sniffed, then took a seat opposite. "No doubt
Giles was there to properly supervise."

Angelica merely continued to smile. She didn't wish to
bother disabusing the woman of the mistaken impression
that her stepbrother had ever been welcomed at Blackstone Abbey. Richard had had Giles's measure even in his
youth. "What is this urgent matter which necessitated a
letter from my stepbrother? Is he not due to return on
Friday?"

"Your brother brings Lord Paden with him on his
return."

Angelica raised one delicately arched black brow, but
made no comment. It took all her efforts to resist a shudder. Baron Paden was a wealthy aging *roué*. Too often over
the past two years Angelica had found him leering at her

since her stepbrother had taken to bringing him to the Park. During his last stay at Edenfield he'd announced he'd decided to set up his nursery and tossed out broad hints that Angelica might be the lucky lady of his choice.

While the legacy which she would inherit from her father in October was small, it afforded her the ability to choose her own destiny, which would not include a coxcomb like Paden, she reflected.

At that moment, Finch entered with the tea tray, staying any comment Angelica might have made. After the butler left and the ladies served themselves, Harriet returned to the message from Lord Edenfield.

Stirring her tea distractedly, Miss Parks avoided Angelica's gaze; then in a rush she announced, "As your guardian, and having only your best interest in mind, Giles accepted Lord Paden's offer of marriage on your behalf. They arrive Friday with a Special License and the marriage shall take place on Saturday."

Angelica returned her teacup to the tray so quickly tea spilled onto the silver surface. In contrast her voice was deadly calm. "Marry Lord Paden? Giles must have taken leave of his senses."

Harriet blushed even as she pursued the unpleasant topic. "Don't be foolish, my dear. Why, the man is rich as Croesus. With no fortune to speak of and being only passably pretty you could never hope to find such an excellent catch as Lord Paden."

In truth, Miss Parks's description of the young lady was far from the mark. Angelica Markham had inherited her mother's violet blue eyes and raven curls which framed a delicate heart-shaped face. Her features were pleasing enough to attract the young gentlemen of the village, but her stepbrother's churlish manners to the neighbors kept any suitors from calling at Edenfield, leaving Harriet with the impression that Angelica's fate would be similar to her own.

Angelica fought to control her anger at the thought that

she could be bought. "Money counts for little when I consider marriage, Harriet." She knew it was a radical idea in a society where a good marriage was the key to financial and social gains, but she would wed only for love. Her mother's marriages had taught Angelica a valuable lesson. The love-match with her father had been happy, while the marriage to the late Lord Edenfield for financial security had proved an extremely difficult experience for the gentle lady.

Bitterly, Harriet interrupted Angelica's thoughts. "That is because you have never known a true lack of funds, being always sheltered by your mother. You think your meager legacy will see you through, but you have no notion of the expenses of being on your own. I warn you, Angelica. You know Giles has ways to make you do his bidding."

Angelica gazed down at her clenched fists. She knew well her stepbrother's methods. He used her affection for the tenants and servants to bend her to his will, often threatening to turn off one or the other if she didn't agree to his wishes.

Looking up she could see the anxiety in Harriet's faded brown eyes, but there was something else there as well—a determination to protect her own position at Edenfield. That meant the lady would see Giles's wishes fulfilled. Angelica couldn't blame Harriet, for without her cousin's support, the woman would be destitute.

Rising, Angelica walked slowly to the door, her mind in a turmoil at her stepbrother's newest betrayal. Upon reaching the portal, she paused, looking back at Harriet. "I am too tired to think about this at the moment. I shall decide what I intend to do on the morrow." So saying, she left the room.

Harriet issued a sigh of relief. That hadn't been so bad. Once Angelica gave the matter some thought, she would see that Lord Paden was likely not such a bad fellow. Sufficient funds went a long way to making a person more palatable. The spinster went and drew a sheet of paper from the small desk near the door. She began making a list of tasks to be accomplished before the wedding. It kept her from thinking about her role in forcing this marriage on Angelica and of the girl's possible fate at the hands of the debauched baron.

Upstairs, Angelica paced the worn Oriental rug in her room. Despite being exhausted, she couldn't stop thinking about what her stepbrother planned. This was no simple dispute about a proposed visit to London or whether she truly needed a new dress. This was a matter that would affect the rest of her life. She was certain that Paden had promised Giles something in return for her hand. Her stepbrother always managed to wring money out of every situation.

She would never agree to marry Lord Paden, and since Angelica knew that Giles would find a way to force her to bend to his will, the only option for her was to leave before he returned. But where would she go? She had no relatives except her stepbrother.

As she paced past the small mahogany secretaire where her mother's herbal book lay open, she noted a slip of pink ribbon hanging from one of the small drawers. Distractedly, she pulled the drawer open and was about to push the ribbon inside when she spied the letters she kept bound by the strip. Pulling out the notes from her godmother, Angelica clutched them to her breast. Lady Longstreet in York was her only hope.

Angelica pulled open a second drawer and began to count the money she'd been saving since before her mother died. She hoped there would be enough to pay her way on the stagecoach all that distance.

It would be her first time away from Edenfield since she'd arrived as a young girl. A thrill of excitement ran through her at the thought of such an adventure. As she glanced up at a nearby window, the fading sunlight made her realize she must begin the preparations for her journey. She scarcely had three days before her stepbrother's return. She would dine with Harriet this evening, then plead fatigue so she might pretend to retire early. If she hurried, she could make the Mail Coach at Croyden which could take her to London this very night, but how would she get to the nearby market town?

The only way would be to take Jenny into her confidence. The maid's brother worked at the Golden Drake in the village and he often took Angelica to Croyden to shop, using the inn's small gig without Giles's knowledge. She was certain he would do so again.

With her decision made, Angelica strode to her wardrobe, pulled out a small portmanteau and began to fill it with clothes for her journey north.

The following morning, Harriet sat before the mirror of her small dressing table, securing her greying hair into a neat knot upon the top of her head. She had a great deal to do this morning, thanks to Giles. The vicar must be informed of the ceremony, and surely Angelica would want flowers in the church.

A sharp knock sounded on her bedchamber door, causing her to start. No one ever came to Harriet's room. The servants went to Angelica for any household problems, and Giles had reduced the staff to such a degree that no one had a personal maid. Tugging a plain white muslin cap over her hair, Harriet rose and called for the visitor to enter.

Finch shuffled into the room, his bristling grey brows drawn together in a marked frown. "Miss Parks, Mrs. Brown came to bring Miss Markham a basket of fresh meadowsweet this mornin' and I went to inform the young miss knowin' she likes to handle her own herbs, but she's not in her room."

Harriet shrugged, unconcerned as she moved to her desk to retrieve her list of things to be done. "You know how Angelica is forever out and about. Put the herbs in the stillroom and tell her when she returns from wherever she has gotten to.''

"Miss Markham would never go off without a servant, and all the maids are busy preparing for the wedding. What's more, her bed hasn't been slept in and her wardrobe is nearly empty." There was a look of censure in the old man's eyes as he stared accusingly at Miss Parks. The servants were well aware that Miss Markham had no wish to become the bride of Lord Paden and that Harriet was aiding her cousin by arranging matters so the wedding could take place immediately upon the gentlemen's return.

Panic ran riot in Harriet's breast. Had Angelica chosen to run away to avoid this forced marriage, for there was no other way to think of the matter. The possibility had never occurred to Harriet, Angelica being without funds or relatives save her slender tie to the viscount.

As the full import of the crisis struck her, Harriet staggered to a wingback chair which stood in front of the fireplace. "I shall be turned out of Edenfield as soon as Giles returns and finds her gone. I shall be homeless."

Finch watched the lady sink dejectedly into the chair. He was torn, his need to be loyal to the viscount, sympathy for the destitute Miss Parks and a genuine affection for Miss Markham warring in him. "Perhaps she will return before his lordship does." But he didn't believe it. Still, he worried about the young lady being all on her own. It was a wicked world out there.

Shaking her head, Harriet wailed, "Where can Angelica have gone, Finch? You know as well as I she has no one to take her in." Harriet racked her brain for where the girl might have fled. There was still the slimmest chance that she might be found and returned to Edenfield, thus saving Harriet's place.

Thinking it best that Miss Markham should be found,

Finch said, "As to that, Miss Markham gets mail regularly from someone in York."

Harriet jumped to her feet. "Yes, I believe you are right. She has a godmother. That is where she would go, but I cannot go to retrieve her. I haven't any funds to pay for the stagecoach, and there is not a single horse to be had in the stable."

The butler stood quietly thinking about the matter. He didn't wish to see Miss Angelica married to Lord Paden, but neither did he wish to see poor Miss Parks tossed out of the Park. Then he was struck by a thought that was perhaps the answer.

"There is one person who would go and bring Miss Markham back and never utter a word of slander against her."

A look of hope leapt into Harriet's brown eyes. Grabbing the old man's hands, she demanded, "Who, Finch, tell me who?"

"Why, Lord Blackstone, miss. I hear he is at the abbey."

"Blackstone! Has age made you addlepated? Of all the harebrained notions to send a rake after an innocent miss. Why, I would as likely send a fox to gather the eggs in the morning."

"But, Miss Parks, only think. Miss Markham and his lordship are old friends. Likely, he sees her in the light of a younger sister. And even if he don't, Lord Paden might think him escorting the lady so improper that he'll withdraw his offer, him being . . ." Finch allowed his voice to trail off, not wishing to voice his opinion of the baron to his betters.

Harriet wrung her hands. She must at least make some attempt to get Angelica back. Giles would perhaps understand her turning to Lord Blackstone at a time like this. Hadn't Angelica indicated they were all great friends in their youth? Yes, she would do it. "Very well, Finch, I am for Blackstone Abbey."

* * *

Richard Thorne, the fifth Earl of Blackstone, groaned at the pounding in his head even as it lay on his own pillow. He'd drunk far too much brandy the evening before, and now he was suffering the effects.

Easing back the covers, he dropped his legs over the side of the huge bed and sat up. The pounding increased. Where the devil was Sanders with that potion he concocted, now when his master needed it most?

The earl stood slowly, then pulled his banyan over his nightshirt. The abbey was always cold, even during the summer. Having given the cord two vigorous pulls to summon his valet, he staggered to an oversized Flemish beech wing chair which had comfortably seated three of the previous four earls. He carefully propped his aching head upon one of his long white hands and awaited some relief.

Within minutes the door opened to reveal his lordship's gentleman. Sanders carried a tray which held a small pewter mug and a large can of steaming hot water. "Good morning, sir. You are up exceedingly early."

His lordship made no comment, merely taking the proffered cup and gratefully downing its contents. After several minutes, he inquired, "What is the time?"

"Half past eleven, sir."

Richard groaned again. Why hadn't he taken advantage of Yardley's invitation? He would have been entertained well into the night by one of the Fashionable Impures that his old friend had invited to his hunting box and wouldn't have been plagued with this cursed headache. But he hadn't felt the slightest twinge of lust at the thought of the painted lightskirts his friend had listed among his guests. The demimondes of Society no longer held the allure they once had. Maybe he was getting old.

"Do you ride this morning?" Sanders was quietly going about the business of laying out the earl's shaving supplies.

"Despite my aching head, I must. I promised my steward

I would see the improvements he's made. He'd never forgive me if I left without seeing his efforts, despite the fact I trust him implicitly." Surprisingly, the earl had been looking forward to the meeting with the man who managed his estates. He'd recently fallen into conversation with an old friend of his father's who'd made some excellent suggestions about livestock management, a topic until now he'd rarely considered. He'd been anxious to hear the bailiff's opinion of the ideas.

Richard carefully edged his head around to gaze out the window to see the weather. It was a sunny day. He wasn't certain, but he thought his head was starting to feel better as long as he didn't try to move about too much.

"After the inspection, where are we off to, my lord? Are we for Lord Yardley's box or to the Middletons's house party? There was a rumor in Town that a certain Lady Eliza Hillyard was yours for the askin', my lord, and she is to be present at the marchioness's gatherin'. An heiress of some fifty thousand, they say."

Richard snorted, sending another frisson of pain through his head. He applied his fingertips to his temples which gave him some ease. "When have you ever seen me in pursuit of an innocent female, Sanders? I have too often been the object of scheming chits interested only in my title or fortune to subject someone else to such treatment."

"My lord, you are unduly harsh in regard to young ladies. You are handsome, intelligent and always well turned out. Can you not believe that a lady could love you for yourself?" Sanders frowned, for he was beginning to fear that the dowager countess was correct and Lord Blackstone would never marry.

Rising, Richard slowly moved across the room to sit at his shaving table. "You are too much of a romantic, Sanders. Were I sixty, and a pudding bag to boot, I would still be considered an eligible *parti* by the matchmaking mamas of the *ton.*"

Sanders fell silent as he began to lather the earl's lean

face. The handsome young peer had grown quite jaded over the last few years.

Some thirty minutes later as the valet helped the earl into a green superfine coat, a knock sounded at the chamber door. The earl called, "Come."

Bagwell, a former soldier, was butler at the abbey. He cleared his throat and stood ramrod straight as he stepped into the earl's bedchamber. "My lord, you have a visitor, a lady."

Richard's hand paused as he buttoned his jacket over a simple green- and white-striped waistcoat. He would have thought that his reputation was sufficiently black to keep the local misses from venturing to his door, but boredom spurred him to ask, "Is she pretty?"

"Got teeth, my lord."

Richard frowned, not taking his meaning. "Teeth?"

"Great rabbity teeth. The lady could eat a fig through a picket fence and not lose a seed, as they say, my lord." Bagwell shook his head as if to rid himself of the image. "Says she is a Miss Parks from Edenfield Park, here on an urgent matter."

Despite the close proximity of the two large estates, there had been little communication between the families. The one link during the current era had been the scrawny little girl he'd befriended years earlier. A smile curved his lips as he remembered little Angel Markham and the summer days fishing in the stream between the estates, the excitement of the child when she'd caught her first greyling.

Heavens, Angel must be grown and married by now. Richard tried to remember if he'd heard such, but he rarely took note of the happenings in the neighborhood.

Frowning, he was curious as to who Miss Parks was. There was only one way to find out. "Very well, Bagwell. Take her to the Yellow Saloon and serve her some refreshments. I shall be there momentarily."

The butler left and Richard allowed Sanders to arrange his blond hair in the Brutus fashion which he usually favored. Satisfied with his appearance, the earl went to see what the unknown Miss Parks wanted.

He entered the Yellow Saloon and discovered a woman of rather advanced age, and markedly protruding teeth, anxiously awaiting him. She rose from the gold damask sofa where she'd been seated and came to him. "Lord Blackstone, I do apologize for this intrusion so early, but I am desperate. We have never met, but I am Miss Parks from Edenfield and I have come to beg your assistance."

Richard's brows rose. There was nothing he disliked more than overly dramatic women. There had been the widowed Lady Winters, who'd sworn she'd throw herself in the Thames if he didn't marry her, and the actress Daisy Lovelace who'd declared she'd kill herself if he didn't buy her an emerald necklace to match her eyes. Neither had resorted to such drastic measures when presented with an expensive diamond bracelet and an introduction to a new protector.

In a rather bored tone, the earl suggested, "Pray, be seated, Miss Parks, and tell me what might be this desperate situation that concerns me."

Harriet eyed the rake as she pulled a handkerchief from her reticule. Dark blond hair framed a handsome angular face. He was elegantly dressed for the country in green coat, tan buckskins and gleaming boots. Despite his marked air of boredom, she found him to be the sort of dangerously attractive man to touch a young lady's heart, but there was nowhere else she could turn.

"My lord, I must take advantage of your long-standing friendship with Miss Angelica Markham and beg you to help that lady."

Richard did some quick calculating and estimated that Angel would be about nineteen or twenty years old. Was she now one of those flighty creatures that cluttered all the fashionable ballrooms of London? Had the skinny girl grown into an antidote, with little conversation and a great deal of ambition to capture a title and fortune? Was this some ruse on the ladies' part to trap him into making an offer on the grounds of old acquaintance? Women were so very predictable.

"In what way do you need my help? I am expected at Lord Middleton's estate in Lincolnshire by the end of the week and have estate business before I depart." The earl gazed down, inspecting the shine on his Hessians. He wondered what Sanders's secret was for achieving such a high gloss.

Harriet felt her face warm. It was clear that he had no intention of bestirring himself to help her or Angelica. Standing abruptly, she said, "Lord Blackstone, I knew you to be a notorious rakehell when I came, but I had not heard you could be so lacking in honor as to abandon an old friend."

Richard's boredom was replaced by an immediate surge of anger. For all his amorous dalliances, he'd never crossed the line of what was proper for a gentleman. He rose and stared down his nose at Miss Parks. "Madam, you may be sure I have never turned my back on any friend in need. If Miss Markham is truly in trouble, then I should know the details before I can decide this for myself."

Harriet realized she must have wounded his pride, a very good sign that he was more honorable than she'd thought. She rushed to explain while she had his full attention. "Miss Markham received an important letter from her brother, the nature of which must remain private. In a foolhardy manner, she decided to flout his wishes and ran away last night. Sir, she will be ruined, for she is traveling by common stage without a proper maid."

Holding her breath, Harriet waited to hear what his lordship would say. If her new impression of his lordship was correct, then he would do her bidding.

"In what direction is the young lady traveling?"

Harriet's knees grew weak with relief, for it seemed he would go after the girl. "I believe she is going north, sir, to York to the residence of a Lady Longstreet."

Richard knew he was every kind of fool to be involving himself in this matter. Why, he hadn't even seen the chit in over six years, but it rankled him that this aging spinster had found him lacking the one principle that all true gentlemen prized, honor. "Very well, I shall leave at once and return Miss Markham to you to protect her good name. But pray that having one with my reputation as her rescuer does not do more harm than good."

" 'Tis a chance I must take, my lord."

The earl strode from the room shouting for his breakfast and his man, leaving Harriet with high hopes that Angelica would be back at Edenfield long before Giles and Lord Paden arrived.

Chapter Two

The York stagecoach swayed and bounced its way along the Great North Road at a lumbering pace. The weather had held fine and the roads were dry, but the vehicle was slowed under the weight of four interior passengers and eight on the top, plus a great number of portmanteaus and trunks.

Angelica gazed out the window, enjoying the passing countryside, confident now that no one from Edenfield was pursuing her. The first night of her journey proved uneventful, but nerve-racking. She'd boarded the Mail Coach at Croyden near midnight, expecting at any moment to be hailed by someone in her stepbrother's employ.

After arriving at the Bull and Mouth Inn in Picadilly, she counted her remaining funds and realized her money would not permit further travel by the expensive Mail. She took a hackney to Holburn where she spent what little remained of the night at the George. Tired from lack of sleep, but determined to escape her stepbrother, she'd taken the first York stage north the following morning.

Having been on the road for nearly two days, and having gotten a good night's sleep at last, she was beginning to enjoy herself. The letters from Lady Longstreet were tucked safely in her portmanteau in the boot of the coach; Angelica hoped that none at Edenfield would remember her mother's old school friend. But even if they did, she would be at Longstreet Manor long before anyone overtook her. Still, would the baroness be able to protect her?

A burst of laughter sounded from the passengers on the roof, intruding on Angelica's thoughts. She wished she could ride on top, for she could have saved half the fare, but the two females presently occupying seats outside were not proper ladies. Not wishing to draw undue attention to herself, she shared the hard wooden seats inside with a reed-thin solicitor's clerk, a farmer's aging wife and her young son. The child slept soundly beside Angelica while clutching a small carved frigate.

The horn blasted from the guard to alert the inn of the arrival of the stagecoach, and it woke the young lad. He yawned and stretched before asking his mother when they would arrive in York, a question that dominated Angelica's mind as well. The woman shushed him, then said they would arrive before dark.

As the coach drew to a halt, Angelica could see the ostlers rushing out to change the team. The clerk made a hurried trip into the inn, but knowing the stop was of a short duration the ladies decided to wait until they stopped for a meal.

Within minutes the clerk returned, clutching the small brown leather satchel he carried, and again sat with his back to the horses. The man had barely settled himself when the coachman called, "Gentlemen, take your seats."

The coach door opened a second time as a large man with greying hair and beard, in the garb of a vicar, climbed in and took a seat beside the clerk. He smiled at the other passengers.

"Good morning, good morning, such a beautiful day to

be traveling, is it not? I am the Reverend Mr. Albert Firth, of Overton." His manner was so amiable that one couldn't resist returning his pleasant smile.

As the coach rolled out of the inn yard, the vicar leaned forward and tweaked the young boy's cheek. "Fine looking lad you have there, Mrs. . . ."

"Greenleaf, sir, and this 'ere is Paul. We're from Greenleaf Farm near York."

"Pleasure to make your acquaintance, ma'am." He then looked at the clerk in a friendly manner. "First time on the York Stage, Mr. . . ."

"Morris, vicar. No, for I travel a great deal for my employer. I'm on my way to deliver papers of some importance to the Marquis of Kerby." The man puffed out his thin chest as if to show he was a person of some importance among the humble company.

Angelica, having dressed in her mother's black traveling grown and veiled bonnet, suddenly found herself the object of the vicar's kind gaze. She'd donned the widow's garb to make it less improper for her to travel unaccompanied as well as to disguise her face, but now she must play the part of the mourning spouse.

"My dear lady, death is a natural part of the cycle of life. God has willed it so. I grieve for your loss, Mrs—"

Guiltily, Angelica uttered her mother's maiden name, "Ansley, sir, and thank you."

"Was it your dear husband who passed?"

Angelica nodded, hesitating to speak. She was at a loss for words, her thoughts racing for something to say; then her gaze lit upon the small wooden frigate. "He was lost at sea, Mr. Firth."

Mr. Morris, being in a particularly dull job, had often engaged in dreams of inheriting a fortune and traveling. To that end, he read the papers religiously to keep abreast of the news around the world. He eyed her suspiciously. "Haven't read of any vessels going down in recent weeks."

"That is likely true, sir. His ship sank over a year ago,

but I was only just notified so I thought it correct to engage in the proper mourning from the time I learned of the tragic event." Angelica struggled not to smile. Even with her face behind the veil, she was certain he would know she was amused by fabricating such a tale.

"It were sharks, weren't it?" Young Paul gazed at her with bloodthirsty interest.

"Sharks?" Angelica had trouble keeping her voice steady.

"Yea, what got yer 'usband. Me brother's a sailor, and he says the ocean is full of 'em. A man can't put 'is toe in the water what it don't get bitten—"

"Paul," Mrs. Greenleaf snapped, "mind your manners, young man. 'Tis not a proper thin' to be speakin' of to poor Mrs. Ansley."

Angelica was thankful when the vicar asked to see Paul's wooden toy, for she was certain she couldn't have answered without laughing. She didn't know what had put her in such a lighthearted mood. Perhaps it was finally being away from her stepbrother's tyranny.

Richard tooled his curricle at a spanking pace up the turnpike. He knew he was getting close to the York stage, for the tollgate keeper said it had passed barely an hour prior. He was surprised to find himself in such good spirits considering he'd spent the last two days chasing after Angel, but in truth, he'd been rather amused by her ingenuity.

At Croyden he'd learned that the young lady must have disguised herself as a widow since that was the only person who'd taken the Mail Coach to London the previous evening. But at the Bull and Mouth, the lady had hired a hackney and disappeared into the night. He'd gone at once to the Swan with Two Necks, which was the point where the Mail Coaches going north started, but there he could find no trace of a widow or any other who answered to his vague description of Angel. Half a day had been wasted questioning the inn's numerous ostlers before he reasoned she might have gone by stagecoach instead.

At Holburn he'd found her trail again, but night had fallen and he decided to treat himself to a good dinner before making an early start of it in the morning. After all, the young lady wasn't in any real physical danger traveling by stagecoach; her widow's disguise would protect her from the slights of a female traveling alone.

Presently about to run her to ground, he wondered if he'd recognize Angel after all these years. He recollected a plain, thin child with leaves and grass tangled in her black braids, racing across the meadow to the stream where he'd awaited her. Then he remembered she'd had the most amazing eyes—large, inquisitive and the most unusual shade of violet-blue. He would know those eyes anywhere.

As the curricle raced round the curve, the village of Wansford came into view. Tooling into town, he ignored the stares that his rapid pace drew. Within minutes, he spied the large coaching inn, its yard cluttered with vehicles, but the black and red stagecoach loomed above the smaller carriages. Richard reined his team to a trot, then deftly entered the inn-yard gate where he called for someone to walk his team.

Within minutes the earl stood in the noisy taproom of the White Rose. The innkeeper seeing a gentleman of some consequence enter, hurried forward. "Would ye be wantin' a private parlor, my lord?"

"Not at present. I wish to be escorted to the room where the stagecoach passengers are dining."

The innkeeper merely nodded his balding head and led his guest into the rear of the inn, making no comment on the unusual request. He'd been owner of the White Rose for twenty years, and he'd learned you didn't question the fits and starts of the Quality and do well in business. He gestured at the door, then left the gentleman to his affairs.

Richard halted in the arched doorway to the public dining room. He was surprised at how crowded the table was. Only four women were among the boisterous group. His gaze came to rest on the back of a shapely feminine form dressed all in black. She bent over to speak to a small child. Her raven black hair was bound in a neat chignon at the nape of her slender neck. A neck which looked excessively kissable.

When that last thought popped unbidden into his mind, he was appalled. This was little Angel, not some lightskirt. What was he thinking of? But as his gaze swept over her, he realized she was certainly no longer a child.

One of the men at the table glanced over and spied Richard. Taking in the elegance of his attire, the fellow assumed him to be a gentleman recently down on his luck, reduced to traveling by common stage. "Best take a seat and eat, sir. The coachman won't wait for anyone. I suspect he'd even leave the likes of Prinny to keep to his schedule."

A tall man at the opposite end of the table added, " 'Tis fortunate the prince don't travel by stagecoach or they'd have to leave half the passengers behind to accommodate a man of his girth."

A murmur of laughter went round the table, for while none had ever personally seen the Prince of Wales, caricatures of the stout regent abounded.

The earl never took his eyes from Angelica as he said, "My good man, you had best have a care about mentioning the royal gentleman's size. Even the illustrious Brummell lost favor for commenting on such."

Like the others at the table, Angelica turned to observe the visitor. As recognition dawned, a radiant smile lit her face and she rose.

The tall man failed to note Richard's attention was engaged elsewhere and responded to the newcomer's banter. "Aye, but I'd never be reckless enough to say it to his face as I hear the Beau did."

Richard experienced a sudden tightening in his chest

at the welcoming expression on Angel's beautiful face. It touched him far more than the most alluring smile ever sent his way. She was genuinely happy to see him. But as he stood mesmerized by her, he realized he could no longer think of her as a little hoyden racing over the countryside. The plain but engaging child was gone, replaced by a woman of extraordinary beauty and appeal—this wasn't his little Angel, this was Miss Angelica Markham. She was an intriguing and desirable woman. Just the sort to engage his interest. A strong yearning to see that sleek black hair spilled across a pillow filled him.

"Rich— Lord Blackstone, how delightful to see you again after all these years." Then a slight frown touched her brow as his presence suddenly seemed suspicious to her. "Why are you here?"

The room had grown quiet. All the travelers seemed interested in hearing the answer to Angelica's question. Richard stepped forward and lowered his voice even as he took note of her temptingly curved pink lips. "I have come for you. Perhaps you would accompany me to a place where we might converse in private. I believe the innkeeper will provide such a room."

Angelica's back went rigid as the earl's hand closed on her elbow, but her curiosity won out and she didn't resist as he led her from the room. She'd been so glad to see him until reason told her he wasn't there by coincidence. She allowed him to lead her a short distance into the hall; then she halted, refusing to go any farther with the man who'd come to bring her home.

"I won't go back, Richard."

"Oh, but you will, my dear. I haven't come all this way to return empty-handed."

He crossed his arms over his broad chest and leaned back against the wall, his mouth quirking in the slightest suggestion of a confident smile. His eyes swept her up and down with a look which made Angelica's heart hammer.

It was clear by that look that he usually got what he wanted, especially with women. She tried to gather her thoughts.

"How could you agree to be a party to my stepbrother's plans?"

"I know nothing of why you and Giles have quarreled, nor do I care. Your Miss Parks has requested—nay demanded—that I save you from your own impetuous nature. So here I am, your knight to the rescue."

She was amazed at the change in him. He was taller and more athletically built than she remembered. His ruggedly handsome face had thinned and the features had become more angular, but it was the look in his amber eyes which struck her the most. Gone was the boyish eagerness and vulnerability she remembered. Instead she gazed up at a man who was everything rumor said: a cynical, jaded rake. What had Harriet been thinking to send such a man after her?

"The armor is a bit tarnished of late," she snapped.

"True, but all it needs is a little polishing by the right lady." The earl grinned at her in such a manner that her knees felt weak.

Turning away from him, she noted a plump maid who was eyeing Lord Blackstone with interest as she wiped a table in the taproom. Angelica looked back at Richard, gesturing toward the servant. "I believe we have just the lady for the task."

Richard gave a soft laugh. "The rumors about me must be loathsome if you think I have stooped to romancing servants."

"Romancing! Is that what you call what you have been doing over the past few years? I do believe they have another name for it." Her violet-blue eyes glinted with outrage.

"Never mind what I have been engaged in over the years. Are you ready to leave?" Somehow Richard didn't like the idea of Angelica knowing all the sordid details of his life.

The anger disappeared from her face, replaced by a look of determination. "I believe I told you that I am not going back with you." Angelica turned as if to leave him.

Annoyed with her continued defiance, the earl reached out and grabbed her arm, liking her softness despite his best intentions. "I swore to return you to Mrs. Parks. You are going, if I have to carry you to my curricle."

Richard and Angelica were so engaged in their dispute that neither was aware of Mrs. Greenleaf, Paul, the reverend and Mr. Morris standing a few feet away and observing the growing argument.

The vicar cleared his throat. "Mrs. Ansley, is there a problem?"

Giving them his haughtiest look, Richard allowed his hand to drop from Angelica's arm. "I am the Earl of Blackstone and this is a private matter, sir."

Angelica suddenly realized she would need assistance to prevent Richard from forcing her into his carriage. She would have to invent some tale, or they would succumb to the power of Richard's title. She moved toward them, her hands extended to the Reverend Mr. Firth. "Sir, I need your help."

Grey brows arched, the vicar eyed his lordship warily. "What can I do, Mrs. Ansley?"

"Who the devil is Mrs. Ansley, sir? You are addressing Miss Markham." Richard found the situation had suddenly gotten out of hand. Angelica shot him a cunning look that suddenly made him wary.

"Reverend, his lordship is determined to spirit me away to Gretna Green and force a marriage upon me."

Forgetting himself, Richard barked, "Angel!"

"I say, my lord," the vicar sputtered, "I am uncertain what is happening here, but you cannot think we shall stand by and allow you to take Mrs. Ansley—er, Miss Markham—against her will."

Mr. Morris nervously eyed the earl. "I shall. None of my business. He can do as he likes."

Mrs. Greenleaf stepped around Angelica, tugging Paul with her, and gazed at the earl with interest, thinking him a handsome young sprig. "I believe there is much 'ere we don't know about what is 'appenin'. Why, for instance, do you call 'er Miss Markham when she introduced 'erself as Mrs. Ansley in the coach?"

Richard, who'd been stunned by Angelica's prevarication, swept the farmer's wife a bow, then gave her his most engaging smile. "Ah, I would say you are a lady of great intelligence, madam."

"Don't try charmin' me, sir. I was born at night, but not last night. I don't know much about anything, but I've raised five boys and four girls. Experience 'as taught me to question 'alf of what I see and most of what I 'ear."

With a wicked grin at Angelica, Richard turned his attention on Mrs. Greenleaf. So, little Angel wanted to play games—well, he would give her a taste of her own medicine. "Very wise, madam. Have no doubt that you have just heard a great farrago of nonsense from the young lady. Miss Markham, for that is her true name, is my ward. This is the fourth time she has run away from school. I suspect she is going to meet her dancing master in Gretna."

Angelica stamped her foot. "That is the greatest hummer, sir. You have not even seen me in the last six years."

"Only because you have been at school." In an undertone to the farmer's wife, he added, "Fortunately, the headmistress of the school caught her the other three times and spared me having to chase after the tiresome chit." Richard struggled not to laugh as he watched the outraged expression on Angelica's lovely face.

Clutching his satchel to his chest, the solicitor's clerk nodded his head. "I knew that tale of a husband lost at sea was a take-in. I think the gentleman is speaking the truth."

At that moment, the coachman bellowed in the inn yard. "Gentlemen, take your seats."

The hallway was suddenly filled with stage passengers pouring out of the dining room and hurrying to get back on board the coach. Mrs. Greenleaf gave Angelica one last look of disappointment, then grabbed Paul's hand and hurried away. Mr. Morris sniffed as if a bad odor were present, then followed.

The vicar sighed, looking first to Angelica and then at the earl. "I am not certain what the truth is here, but I suspect it is somewhere in between. I would only say, Miss Markham, you should go back to where you belong and you, my lord, should make certain that the lady comes to no harm. I fear I must go."

"Very wise advice, sir." Richard bowed to the departing clergyman, then stepped into Angelica's path as she tried to follow. "No, Angel, you cannot go with the stagecoach."

"Don't call me Angel! That is a name reserved for my old friend Richard, but it seems he is dead and gone, killed by a libertine named *Lord Blackstone.*"

Having said that, Angelica turned her back on her former friend, and attempted to walk away, but the earl again grabbed her arm, leading her to the inn yard. She wasn't certain what bothered her more, that her old friend had come to take her back to Edenfield or how much she liked the feel of his hand on her arm. It didn't truly matter, because at the first opportunity, she would escape from Lord Blackstone and his strange effect on her.

Chapter Three

Angelica angrily tied the ribbon to her bonnet, leaving the veil thrown back. There was no point in trying to disguise herself now that she'd been found, and no amount of pleading would convince the coachman that she was anything other than what Lord Blackstone accused her of being—a flighty runaway. She sat in the earl's curricle, knowing she must bide her time for the right opportunity to escape. She watched Lord Blackstone arguing with the stagecoach driver over the matter of her portmanteau. At last a coin changed hands; then the man grudgingly opened the boot to retrieve her bag.

Within a matter of minutes, the coachman took his position on the box. With a loud jingle of the harness, the driver called to his team, "Walk on and be lively 'bout it, lads. We're late." The York stage rolled out of the yard filling Angelica with a sense of despair.

The earl strode toward the carriage, a satisfied smile on his handsome face. Angelica schooled her features into a haughty mask and stared straight ahead. She wouldn't say another word to the man who was betraying her in this unfeeling manner.

Richard shoved the portmanteau under his seat, taking note of Angelica's rigid posture and dark expression. Settling beside the irate miss, he took up the reins and ordered the ostler to stand clear. He was amazed at how much he disliked the idea of her being out of countenance with him, but felt he was doing the proper thing in returning her home. With a sidelong glance at her beautiful face, he realized he would enjoy the task of teasing her out of her vexation. Leisurely, he tooled out of the village.

"There is no need to look as if I were taking you to Tyburn tree, my dear."

Silence greeted his teasing remark. When they were younger such a statement would have brought a smile to her lips.

"Ah, so I am now to be punished for my efforts by being treated to silence." Richard chuckled. "I am truly amazed that women believe it is punishment to cease their inane chattering for an extended length of time." He took a quick glance to see if he'd annoyed her sufficiently to induce her to speak. The muscles in her jaw clenched and unclenched, but still she failed to comment on his provoking remark. Treating her silence as a challenge, he was determined to bring her out of the doldrums before they reached London.

For the next hour or more, Richard kept up a steady flow of commonplaces about the weather, the countryside they drove through and people they passed on the road. Still Angelica sat mutely staring straight ahead, refusing to respond to him.

At last tired of the sound of his own voice Richard challenged, "I see I shall have to resort to some drastic measure to get you to speak to me. Now, what would do the trick?" He thought for several minutes then a smile tipped his mouth. "Perhaps a kiss on those pouting lips might elicit a response?"

Angelica gasped, gazing at him with a mixture of dismay and anger. Yet within her there was also a curiosity at how his lips would feel pressed to hers. Shocked at her wanton thoughts, she snapped, "You wouldn't dare, my lord."

"Hark, the lady again speaks." The earl chuckled, then countered, "Of course I would dare, my dear. After all, did you not accuse me of being a libertine? The art of lovemaking is what we libertines excel in."

Angelica's heart hammered as she noted his gaze lingering on her mouth. She forced herself to look back to the road, wondering how the young man she knew could have changed so much and why the very thought of his kiss made her warm all over.

Almost as if he'd read her mind, the earl said, "You know I am still the same Richard you knew, Angel. Perhaps a bit older and a bit more jaded in the ways of the world, but deep inside is still the person who showed you how to fish, who dried your tears when you scraped your elbows and who taught you to ride my horse."

Angelica looked curiously at the man beside her as he drove the carriage. He was devastatingly handsome in a russet brown coat and tan buckskins, his black beaver hat set at a rakish angle over his blond hair. He was the epitome of the polished gentleman. Was it possible that all his good qualities were still there beneath that heartless sophisticated veneer? Despite his avowed disinterest, would he help her if he knew what Giles had planned? She decided to test his claim.

"If you are still my friend, I beg you, take me to York."

"Because I *am* your friend, I'm taking you home. I'm surprised that you are fleeing from a confrontation with your stepbrother. You were never wont to be faint of heart before."

"Nor am I now, but you have made it plain that you care not what Giles and I are at odds about."

"I begin to think that I was hasty in my remarks. Do you

wish to tell me what has you so determined to journey to York?"

With a sigh, Angelica said, "Giles has arranged for me to be wed."

Richard felt a strange twist in his gut. He really shouldn't have eaten in such a hurry earlier, he thought. So Angel was fleeing a marriage of convenience. While he had no desire to marry at present, he could understand one's reluctance to becoming leg-shackled. But it was different for females, wasn't it? Angelica was well past the age when young ladies wed. He knew girls just out of the schoolroom often held foolish notions about marriage, but he thought her beyond the age to be so missish about such matters. When he responded his voice was heavy with sarcasm. "Ah, I see. You, no doubt, cherished youthful visions of a love-match. Surely you are far past that naive nonsense."

"I should have known I was wasting my breath telling a hardened rake my dilemma. Likely, you shall never experience love because you, sir, are a heartless wretch, squandering your life debauching London's young females. How could I have expected any help from such a quarter?" Angelica angrily turned as far to her left as the curricle would allow, knowing she'd been unconscionably rude, but she didn't care. He was an unfeeling brute who deserved what he got.

Suddenly she was struck by an idea. If only she could make Richard sufficiently angry, he might actually put her down at the next inn.

The young lady's bitter words touched a nerve deep inside Richard, causing him to snap, "I'll have you know I have never debauched any young female."

"Oh! Then when we next stop I shall put out a hue and cry to all within the sound of my voice to lock up their grandmothers, to protect them from unwanted advances since that is where your interest lies." She watched his reaction hopefully.

At first Richard frowned; then his amber eyes began to

twinkle with amusement. "Don't think you can provoke me into doing something rash, my dear. No matter how sharp your tongue, I fully intend to keep a close eye on you until we reach Edenfield."

Angelica sagged back against the leather seat in disappointment. Her thoughts rampaged from one idea to another on how best to escape from Richard and his mission to usher her back into Giles's clutches. If making him angry didn't work, perhaps her best chance was to lull him into believing she'd accept her fate, make him think she was willingly going back. They would have to stop soon for the night. If she played her part right, she might be in York before he knew she was gone. Squaring her shoulders, she began her ploy.

"Richard, I do apologize for my monstrous conduct. My quarrel with Giles has nothing to do with you. You are correct in that I must go back and face him." Angelica's heart hammered. She was certain the earl would know she was prevaricating.

He eyed her closely for several minutes; then a smile lit his face that made Angelica realize why women fell victim to his charms.

"Such a sudden change of heart, my dear. Well, I shall not question it, but I am delighted to see you are the same reasonable young lady I remembered. Now, tell me what you have been doing since we last spent a pleasant afternoon together."

Feeling more confident that she would yet make it to Lady Longstreet, Angelica set out to convince Richard that she was reconciled to returning to Edenfield.

"Finch, we must send someone to Blackstone Abbey to see if they have any news of his lordship." Having come down to the front hall in search of news, Harriet paced in front of the butler, nervously pulling at her handkerchief. Her distraction was so great, she was unaware that her cap sat askew and she wore one black slipper and one brown. " 'Tis nearly two full days since the earl left, and we have heard nothing."

"I'm certain Lord Blackstone will bring Miss Angelica straight home, once he finds her, Miss Parks. There's a great many coaches on the road, so no doubt it's takin' the gentleman a good deal of time to discover her."

"More likely he found himself some flash mollisher to sate his lust, Harriet muttered bitterly to herself. "I should never have asked the likes of him to go."

Finch's brows rose at the cant term for a straw damsel. He wondered where the spinster had come across such language. Despite knowing the remark wasn't meant for his ears, the butler felt the need to defend his lordship. "Not likely Lord Blackstone would be distracted from his mission by some common piece, ma'am."

"Do you think so?" Harriet's face held hope.

"Absolutely, miss. If he got diverted, and I'm not sayin' he did, you can be certain it was some high-flyer or prime article, not a low female."

Harriet wailed, "Oh, Finch, you are—"

The sounds of a carriage drawing up at the door caused the spinster to halt her reprimand. Before the butler could react, the lady dashed to the large oak door and threw it open. The old man heard a loud groan; then the spinster collapsed in a heap.

"Finch!" Lord Giles Edenfield's voice bellowed from outside. "What the devil is this foolish creature doing blocking the door? Get her out of the way!"

The butler rushed forward and lifted Miss Parks by the arms, pulling her limp form to a faded, blue satin sofa against the wall, on which he unceremoniously deposited her. He quickly returned to where the viscount and his guest stood. The visitor, removing his gloves, stared at the lump that was Harriet Parks.

"I say, Giles, didn't know your cousin was a tippler," Lord Paden commented in a bored voice. The gentleman was short and barrel-chested, dressed in a crimson coat with garnet pantaloons giving him the look of an overripe cherry.

"Finch, what is the meaning of this outrage? Has Harriet seen fit to invade my wine cellar?" Giles glared down at the old man. The viscount was tall and lean with dark brown hair framing a hawklike face that held a look of perpetual discontent. His one extravagance was his attire and while he was no dandy, he dressed in the first style of elegance.

"Ain't cup-shot, my lord. Miss Parks fainted." Finch glanced over his shoulder at the lady, very much wishing her to revive. He didn't want to have to be the one to inform his master about the flight of Miss Angelica.

"Fainted! Harriet's never been vaporish. What ails her?" Giles handed his hat and gloves to the butler, then turned to the mirror above where Miss Parks lay to straighten his cravat, hardly sparing a glance for his unconscious cousin despite his question.

Finch silently hoped for a miracle to occur before he had to tell his lordship the truth. A moan from the direction of the sofa seemed an answer to his prayers. He turned to see Harriet Parks put her hand to her head, then shoot up from the sofa as if she'd been fired from a cannon.

"G-Giles, we weren't expecting you until tomorrow." The spinster wavered on her feet as she stood staring at her cousin, the black of her drab gown making her face appear deadly white.

"We finished our business early. Erwin was anxious to see his future bride. Where is Angelica?"

Finch thought Miss Parks was about to swoon again, but at last she squeaked out the word, "Gone."

The viscount frowned. "Gone where?"

Seeing the spinster's face go ashen and her lips quiver, the butler took pity and blurted out, "Went to visit her godmother in York, sir."

"Are you telling me that Angelica left Edenfield and

neither of you attempted to stop her?" An icy cold gaze flicked from spinster to butler then back.

Harriet, at last realizing there was no way to avoid the bare facts, straightened her back even while she began to twist her lace handkerchief. "She never told anyone of her plans. We would certainly have prevented her leaving had we known. But never fear, I have asked your friend, Blackstone, to retrieve her. We were expecting them when you arrived."

"Friend?" Edenfield questioned.

"Blackstone!" Lord Paden roared the word as if he were swearing. "Why the man is not to be trusted with women!"

Giles's mind was racing even as he struggled to control his desire to throttle his foolish cousin. Blackstone was no friend of his, nor had he ever been. What could have given Harriet such an idea? Angelica, no doubt, but he wouldn't allow his stepsister to jeopardize his chance at gaining entry into Paden's business undertakings. If she married the baron, Giles knew he'd eventually be one of the wealthiest men in England. The very thought made him lick his lips in anticipation. But how to cover Harriet's blunder of sending a rake after his tiresome stepsister? He glared at the homely spinster.

Harriet quaked as she took in the fury in the viscount's brown eyes. "I-I thought you and the earl had grown up together."

Lord Paden's face had grown quite red. "Likely the chit is ruined if he's with her. Not a fit wife now."

Desperate, Giles tried to bluster his way past the baron's agitation. "Balderdash! 'Tis like Harriet said, we are all old friends. Why he quite thinks of her as his little sister."

"I cannot think that such a hardened rake would be immune to your sister's beauty over the course of the long journey back from York, no matter the former relationship."

Giles felt certain the baron was correct, for Blackstone's reputation was legend. "Then I say we go after them, for my stepsister's own good. He is likely still chasing after her, what with all the coaches that leave London for York. We shall drive through the night and perchance reach her before Blackstone does."

Paden seemed to ponder this for a few minutes. As visions of the beautiful Miss Markham passed through his mind, he decided he'd waited for her too long to give up now. "Very well, but first we must dine." He was willing to miss his sleep, but not his supper.

Finch, Harriet and Giles issued a collective sigh of relief, all for different reasons. Finch because his master hadn't flown into the boughs and the worst seemed to be over. Harriet because Giles hadn't ordered her from his home, and the viscount because he was certain the baron would marry Angelica before the week was out.

The sky had grown darkly ominous during the long afternoon of travel, but the earl had continued to drive south toward London. As Angel sat telling him of her life at Edenfield, he realized what an innocent she still was. If half of what she said was true, once Giles inherited the title he must have unleashed all his worst qualities. Somehow it seemed wrong to force her into an unwanted marriage. He was tempted to speak to Giles on her behalf, until he realized where his sentimental thoughts were leading him.

By George! Had he taken leave of his senses to be thinking about involving himself in this chit's affairs? After all, such marriages were common in the *ton*. She was nothing to him after all, was she? Innocent females were clearly dangerous to be around, if one always felt this need to protect them.

Angelica interrupted his thoughts.

"When shall we stop for the night?"

Richard knew no respectable inn would allow the pair to put up since she had no maid or companion. They would have to drive straight through, which was probably best for the young lady's reputation after all. He was rather too well known to risk stopping at one of the coaching inns, so he would choose some place small to dine and then they would again head south. Instead of telling Angel, he merely said, "Trumpington is the next village, shall we stop and have supper?"

Angelica's nerves began to tingle. She would now be able to put her plan to work. "I should like that."

Within a matter of minutes they tooled into the small village. To Angelica's surprise and disappointment the earl chose the smaller of the two inns of Trumpington, a rather ancient half-timbered building with little sign of life save one aged ostler sitting by the open door.

As the earl drew his curricle to a halt in front of the establishment, the old man stared like a moonling. Then, when it was clear the vehicle intended to remain there, he struggled to his feet and came to eye the pair. "Are ye certain ye want to stop at the Gray Dove, gov'ner? Quality mostly puts up at the Royal Arms at the other end of the village."

"Quite certain, indeed. See to the horses while the lady and I dine."

Angelica soon found herself in a small taproom filled with local farmers drinking ale. She stood beside the earl, facing the owner and his plump wife who eyed her with suspicion. Noting the dubious look the woman gave her, Angelica realized for the first time the impropriety of traveling with Richard unaccompanied by a female.

The innkeeper, seeing an opportunity for making some quick blunt rather than the unseemly situation, stepped forward. "Sir, how may I serve?"

Thinking it best not to reveal their true names, Richard said, "The name's Black, Mr. Black. As you can see, Mr. . . ."

"Miller, sir."

"Miller, my ward, Miss Smith, and I are in a great hurry and shall only require a meal this evening in a private parlor, if you have such." The earl looked around as if he doubted they would be so lucky as to dine in privacy in the small inn.

The innkeeper glanced nervously at his wife before replying, "Well, sir, Mrs. Miller's a grand cook, and we've a private room for your use, but it'll take us some time to get a proper meal together, not being used to providin' for the Quality and all."

"Very good. We shall wait in the private parlor until our meal is ready."

Angelica, seeing her chance, said, "Perhaps you might show me to a room where I may freshen up and rest until we dine." She gave Richard an innocent smile when he arched one brow.

Mrs. Miller signaled to a small buxom maid who was collecting empty tankards. "Sally, take the young lady up to one of the rooms; then come to the kitchen at once. We've lots to do."

"Mr. Black." Angelica said the name with mockery. "I hope you don't mind my leaving you for a while. I am so fatigued. I shall be down when dinner is served."

Richard bowed. "Miss Smith, rest well."

After the young miss had gone upstairs and the gentleman strolled back out the front door as if he meant to walk about the village, Mrs. Miller sniffed, "If that be a Mr. Black and a Miss Smith, then I'm Queen Charlotte and you're Mad George."

"Hush, Bessie, and get to cookin'. It don't matter if he's Mr. Black or Black Jack the highwayman as long as he pays his shot, and from the looks of him I'd say his pockets are deep. Now, get to the kitchen." The innkeeper took his wife's shoulders and turned her in the right direction before giving her a nudge. Bessie was a bit too moral to his way of thinkin' and he wouldn't allow her to turn away some easy funds for the sake of what was proper.

Upstairs, Angelica plotted to get away from Richard. She went to the window and looked out. The dark clouds blotted out the setting sun. The inn was situated at the edge of the woods, which would make it easy for her to hide, but she suddenly knew a moment's regret. The afternoon in the earl's company had been pleasant despite the circumstances. He'd been utterly charming, telling her amusing tales of his life in Town, although she was certain they'd been greatly edited for her benefit, and he'd seen to her comfort each time they'd stopped to change horses. He'd been like the Richard of old.

Remembering Giles's plans for her, she pushed the pleasant thoughts of Richard from her mind. She had to get away.

Taking a few minutes to refresh herself after the long carriage ride, she then went to the door and listened. Only the low murmur of conversation from the taproom echoed in the hallway. Nervously, she drew the door open and looked out. There was no one about so she quickly tiptoed down the hall toward the backstairs.

As she made her way down the narrow flight, Angelica could hear Mrs. Miller issuing orders in the kitchen. When she reached the last step, she paused to peek around the corner. Sally was busy building up the fire in the oven. Mrs. Miller was slicing meat, all the while complaining to the young maid about the extra work and for such a havey-cavey pair. Neither could see Angelica, so she stepped to the rear door which was near the stairs and exited quietly.

As the back door clicked shut behind her, Angelica felt a rush of exhilaration at having gotten out of the inn unseen. Once she made it to the safety of the woods, Richard would never find her. She didn't dwell on what she would do next, only on getting away from the earl.

In the growing darkness of the impending storm she could see a path which cut through the inn's small rear garden. The trail passed through a wooden arbor heavy with small white roses and disappeared in the woods beyond.

She dashed down the path through the arbor and

straight into the arms of Lord Blackstone, who'd stepped from behind the arch as she rushed headlong for the woods.

His arms closed around her and he pulled her to his hard chest. As he stood holding her close, an amused smile on his handsome face, Angelica was suddenly flooded with the desire to put her arms around his neck. What madness was this?

"Going somewhere, Angel?" His voice sounded husky.

"I-I just thought I might get some air." Something intense flared within her as she felt the warmth of him through her clothes.

"I see, and you thought you might best get some air at a full run."

Feeling she must remove herself from the all too-enticing feel of his arms, Angelica angrily pulled away. "Very well, let there be no more lies. I was trying to get away from you . . . so I might continue my journey to York." The last was said with a sniffle.

Richard held himself in check as he watched her reach up and pluck a flower from the vines growing on the arbor, inhaling its fragrance even as a tear rolled down her porcelain cheek. He was overwhelmed with the desire to again take her in his arms and kiss away dear Angel's tears, but honor forbade it. He wasn't certain he could stop after a few kisses, for she was the most enticing woman he'd found himself in company with.

For once he wished his mother were present to advise him what he should do. Angel should be returned to Edenfield where she properly belonged, but this marriage was so very repugnant to her, how could he be a party to betraying his old friend?

"Angel, I don't—"

Just at that moment Miller came hurrying down the path. "Mr. Black, everythin' is prepared and awaitin' you and Miss Smith in the private parlor."

''We shall be there directly.'' Richard never took his gaze from Angel as she stood with her back to the innkeeper.

After Miller bowed and then disappeared back into the inn, Richard took Angel's hand, drawing her to face him. ''My dear, I think we are both tired and quite famished. Shall we go in and have the supper Mrs. Miller has worked so hard to prepare. You will feel more the thing after you have eaten.''

Richard hoped that was true, for he felt bound by his promise to return Angel to Miss Parks. Perhaps if he found why she was so reluctant to marry, he might better understand and be able to ease her fears. But somehow the idea of Angel being wed left him feeling melancholy.

With a growing sense of uneasiness, he led her back to the inn.

Chapter Four

The innkeeper had made no idle boast of his wife's culinary skills. Dinner in the lone private parlor of the Gray Dove was excellently prepared, if somewhat basic, consisting merely of turtle soup, sliced ham, braised potatoes with dill and peas in cream sauce.

At first there had been an embarrassed silence; then Richard again dominated the conversation with amusing talk of Society, all the while keeping a close watch on Angel. By the time they'd finished their soup, she'd been able to compose herself sufficiently to compliment Mrs. Miller's fare to Sally.

At last left alone with their dessert of apple tarts and thick slices of cheddar, Richard said, "I think we need to speak about your reluctance to return to Edenfield."

Angelica's violet-blue gaze came to rest on Richard. Several raven black curls hung loose from her chignon, dangling seductively about her beautiful face.

"I shan't allow Giles to decide who I marry when I am so close to my majority. *If* I marry it will only be for love."

Richard made a dismissive gesture with his hand before picking up his tankard of home brew. " 'Tis rarely the way for people of our class, my dear." He drank deeply, eyeing her over the pewter cup. Setting the empty vessel back on the table, he leaned back and inquired, "If I might be so bold, may I inquire who Giles has chosen to be your husband?"

Angelica abandoned her half-finished tart. Pushing back her chair, she walked to the mullioned window. Lifting the latch, she pushed it open, needing the fresh air before responding, "Baron Paden."

While Richard had never met the man, Paden's ability to invest wisely was well known throughout the *ton,* where the gentleman had been dubbed Lord Midas. In the eyes of Society, Angel's marriage would have been considered an advantageous one.

Before Richard could comment, Angelica added, "You, no doubt, are acquainted with him from your work in the House of Lords."

For the first time in his life, Richard was embarrassed by his lack of adherence to his duties. Angel naively assumed he'd properly attended to the business of government inherent with a title, while in fact he'd been otherwise amusing himself as he always had since coming to Town.

Irritated to have a mirror held up to his faults, he turned his anger on the one who held the looking glass. Rising, he walked over to stand opposite her. "So, you shun this alliance with one of England's wealthiest lords in favor of what? A life on your own, doing good works and dwindling into spinsterhood, living with that hatchet-faced Miss Parks."

Angelica was certain he was angry with her, but she hadn't a clue why. Tilting her chin upward, she said, "I shall receive a small income from my late father's estate when I am one and twenty in October. I see nothing wrong with settling in a small cottage in the country and doing as I please, my lord."

Richard took a step closer. "Do you think Miss Parks or some other poor female could protect you from the advances of any passing rogue?" So saying, he slid an arm around her waist and drew her to him.

Her heart pounding, Angelica ordered in a hoarse whisper, "Unhand me, sir."

Amber eyes gazed into hers. In a ragged voice, Richard said, "You need a man to protect you, Angel. You are too beautiful for your own good." He then lowered his mouth to hers.

His lips were punishing and angry, yet she found herself responding. A shiver of desire raced through her and she wanted him never to stop, but suddenly he released her, stepping back to stare curiously at her as if they'd never met.

"You see what can happen to innocent young ladies without a proper protector," Richard growled breathlessly. He turned away from her and ran his hands through his blond hair, leaving it tousled like a small boy's. "We shall travel through the night. I must have the hood raised on the curricle for it is likely to rain. Be ready in ten minutes." He stalked from the room without a backward glance.

Angelica stood by the window, her fingers tracing her still throbbing lips. She was certain Richard had kissed her to convince her to marry Lord Paden, but the embrace had had the opposite effect. The very idea of such sweet intimacy with the baron sent a shudder down her spine.

Her thoughts on her old friend were in such turmoil she couldn't clearly define them. All she knew was that as long as Richard intended to force her to go back to Edenfield, she would try to escape him, no matter her feelings. With that thought settled in her mind, she went to prepare herself for their journey.

They traveled through the dark August night with only the carriage lanterns for illumination. With each successive town, fewer windows radiated light as the hour drew near midnight. A soft rain had begun to fall within an hour of their taking to the road, and with each mile they traveled south the storm had increased. Their pace dwindled to a plodding walk on the now muddy road.

A strained silence existed between the pair. On Richard's part, the lack of conversation was due to his anger at his own conduct at the inn. He'd had no business kissing Angel, even less enjoying it as much as he had. Undoubtedly, she thought him an unremitting cad. But then, hadn't he behaved as such by taking advantage of a young lady under his care? He'd violated one of his primary rules about never dallying with an innocent. Pushing thoughts of the alluring lady beside him from his mind, he squinted to see through the curtain of rain.

Angelica's thoughts were on that kiss as well, but along a completely different vein. Despite the angry manner of the embrace, it had left her wanting Richard to kiss her again. Had she merely fallen under the spell of a practiced rake, or did she harbor tender feelings for him?

Sneaking a peek at the earl's face in the golden glow of the lantern, his skin misted with rain, she felt her heart turn in her chest. With the slightest encouragement, she knew she could fall in love with Richard. She forced her gaze back to the road, barely visible through the downpour. She mustn't make that mistake. He saw women as most men saw a good horse—when one took his fancy, he had to possess it, but once he did, he was always looking for another to excite his interest. She wouldn't allow herself to become just another forgotten creature in his stable of women.

"Are you getting wet, Angel?"

Richard interrupted her thoughts. She was surprised how matter-of-fact his voice sounded. "A bit."

"Under your seat is a traveling rug. Pull it out and cover yourself."

Angelica quickly found the rug and spread it over their

feet and legs. Even with the curricle hood up, the rain had left her gown damp and the warmth of the woolen cover was welcome. She sat back wondering how late the hour as they passed an old cottage beside the road, a lantern hanging lit by the door. Was Richard so desperate to be rid of her that he would make them journey all night long?

As they moved slowly southward, the rain lessened to a slow drizzle, but from the carriage lanterns, Angelica could see their vehicle traveled through deep water. Her alarm growing, she was about to voice her concerns when a wheel sank down to the axle and the curricle suddenly dipped to the right. Thrown against Richard, she would have fallen into the water had he not grabbed her even as he struggled with the reins.

"Are you all right, my dear?" The earl's voice was full of concern.

Attempting to right herself, Angelica discovered that the angle of the curricle prevented her from moving away from him. The feel of his muscular limbs against her made her stutter, "I-I am unharmed, but whatever shall we do?"

"Can you hold the ribbons while I get out and see if I can lead the team to pull us out of this hole?" His face seemed barely inches from hers.

"Yes," Angelica replied as she reached for the reins, never taking her gaze from his.

He sat looking back at her in a bemused manner as both their hands held the leather leads; then he seemed to remember himself. He carefully eased out of the carriage, and she slid into his vacated seat, finally stopping when she came to the tilted curricle's side.

Water swirled up near the tops of Richard's Hessians, but he paid little heed, his thoughts were so full of Angel. He was amazed at how her nearness affected him. Not merely with desire, but with an urge to take care of her and protect her. Pushing such disturbing thoughts from him, he trudged to the horses' heads and was about to encourage them onward, when the sounds of rushing water echoed from ahead. He returned and removed a lantern from the carriage, telling Angel to hold the team steady while he inspected the road.

Walking through the darkness, he held the lantern high as the water only got deeper. He stopped and peered into the night. He could barely make out a bridge. Water rushed past the stone structure in a torrent. They'd come to a river which had overflown its banks and they'd get no farther south tonight.

As the water reached his fingertips, he knew it would be dangerous to continue in the direction of the bridge. The rapidly flowing water tugged at his body, trying to draw him downstream. He couldn't risk being swept away and leaving Angelica here alone.

Returning to the carriage where she waited patiently, he told her the news. "The way is flooded, we shall have to go back to find a place to stay for the night."

But when he attempted to move the vehicle, the carriage proved obstinate and remained stuck in the mud. No matter what the earl tried, the team was unable to pull the curricle free. Blaming himself for having continued even in the storm, Richard went back to Angelica. "I'm afraid we are stranded."

Just then the rain returned to a hard downpour, causing Richard to scramble back into the carriage, sliding down the leather seat until the length of his body was against Angelica's. He put his arm on the seat behind her to brace himself, to keep from crushing her. "Forgive me," he muttered with a slight grin.

Angelica knew the slant of the carriage was forcing their close proximity, but that didn't stop the image of being held by him throughout the night. She suspected a night in Richard's arms would be dangerous. "I-I believe we passed a cottage a mile or so back. Shall we unhook the team and see if they will allow us to shelter there?"

"An excellent notion. Stay here while I unhitch the horses." He waded to the rear of the curricle and retrieved an umbrella from the small boot, gave it to Angelica. "When I have the horses turned around, you can ride to this cottage without getting your feet muddy."

Within a matter of minutes the earl had his team free of the traces. He took the carriage rug and placed it on Zephyr's back. Then he lifted Angelica from the curricle. His very strength took her breath away.

Angelica was certain her cheeks were red from the electrifying feel of his arms about her waist and limbs. He lightly tossed her up, and she quickly settled upon the horse's back. She opened the umbrella, thankful for the darkness which hid her blushes. He returned to the carriage one last time and retrieved their portmanteaus.

It seemed an eternity until they reached the cottage where the lantern still glowed its welcome. Richard sat the portmanteaus on the steps before coming to help her down. He remained with his team while Angelica went to knock at the door.

Despite the lateness of the hour, within minutes the latch lifted and a small sleepy-eyed boy of seven or eight with curly brown hair peeked out. "What ye want?"

Too tired to worry about protecting their identity Angelica said, "I am Miss Markham, and that is Lord Blackstone." She gestured to the earl who stood holding his team. "Our carriage has sunk in the mud, and we are stranded. Might we come in?"

The young boy chewed his lower lip for a moment, then called to the earl. "Are ye a real lord?"

"A very wet lord who would like to find a dry place for my horses as well." Richard touched the brim of his hat, which poured a river of water.

Eyeing the animals with interest, the lad seemed convinced there was no danger. He threw open the door for

Angelica. "Sit by the fire, ma'am, whilst I help 'is lordship stable 'is prads."

The boy pulled a hat from a peg by the door, then dashed out into the rain, gesturing for his lordship to follow as he disappeared into the darkness. After the pair left, Angelica picked up the portmanteaus and stepped into the cottage. She called to see if anyone else was at home, but it appeared the young boy was alone, a somewhat shocking circumstance considering his tender age.

Taking the bags, she walked to the center of the large room, then set them on the dirt floor. She was delighted to see a fire on this rainy August night. Thoroughly damp, she welcomed the warmth. Looking around she discovered a small alcove which held a bed with a rough straw mattress, a curtain acted as a door to the tiny room. She opened her bag and retrieved a dry gown and hurried behind the curtain. By the time Richard and the young boy returned, she was seated in front of the fire in an old lilac sprig muslin gown combing her black hair, her wet dress hanging on a chair beside her to dry.

Richard paused on the threshold as he removed his greatcoat, moved by the picture of Angel, her hair loose, smiling at his young companion who'd gone to stand beside her to chatter about his lordship's horses. That was the way she used to smile at Richard long ago, and suddenly he wanted her to look at him in that manner again.

Certain the rain must have reached his brain to be thinking such maudlin thoughts, he tossed his greatcoat across the back of a chair, then turned from the scene to struggle out of his drenched jacket.

Soon he joined the pair by the fire. His wet, lawn shirt clung uncomfortably, but he didn't want to embarrass Angel by removing it. "Miss Markham, allow me to introduce our host, Mr. Daniel Wiggins."

"Right pleased to make yer 'quaintance, miss." Daniel pulled his hat from his head, making his brown curls point forward, then he gave a great sleepy yawn.

Angelica smiled at the lad's formal greeting. Despite the lack of a parent's presence, it was clear he'd been properly brought up. "I'm delighted to meet you, Daniel, but I suggest that you might want to don some dry clothes, or you might catch cold, then return to your bed."

The boy looked to his lordship. Richard nodded his agreement.

"Well, I'll sleep in the loft, and the lady can take the bed." He gestured to the small room where Angelica had changed. "But where'll ye sleep, my lord?"

"Here before the fire." Richard gestured to one of the wooden chairs. Seeing the boy frown, the earl smiled. "Don't worry, I shall make myself comfortable."

Daniel wished the pair good night, and climbed the ladder to the loft. Left alone with Angelica, Richard inquired if she'd taken any harm from her wetting. She quickly assured him she was fine, but urged him to use the small room to don dry clothes.

Richard took his bag and disappeared behind the curtain. Soon he returned in stockinged feet, dry tan buckskins and a shirt, but no cravat. He apologized for his informal attire, but pleaded an insufficient wardrobe to cover their drenching. Placing his Hessians beside the fire to dry, he settled into a chair.

Angelica's gaze trailed to the vee in the earl's lawn shirt which exposed a muscular chest. She was very conscious of his virile appeal, and the blood raced through her veins. With an effort she drew her gaze to the fire. Aware that he was looking at her, she uttered the first thought to come to her mind, "Don't you find it strange that Daniel is here by himself?"

The earl looked curiously about the room. He'd been so conscious of Angel since he'd arrived in the room, that the thought hadn't occurred to him. "Now that you mention it, I do. Perchance his parents went to the village, which young Daniel told me is just beyond the bridge we didn't reach, and got stranded on the other side."

Angelica nodded her head, not having thought of such. "Yes, that is likely, for I cannot imagine what else would keep a responsible parent away at night."

Several possibilities of an illegal nature occurred to Richard, but he didn't mention them to Angelica. "Daniel tells me the village of Throcking is a mile or so beyond the river. That means we are in Hertfordshire."

"Speaking of the river which we were unable to cross, what shall we do on the morrow?"

"If the rain stops soon . . ." Richard paused as he heard the latch on the cottage door lift. He turned to see a man dressed in an overlarge black cape and a wide brimmed hat which left his face obscured enter the cottage, a pistol tucked into the front of his pants.

Thinking they'd stumbled into the cottage of a highwayman, Richard rose and grabbed the dueling pistol he always carried in his greatcoat when he traveled, praying the powder was still dry. He leveled it at the man demanding, "Who are you?"

"I might be askin' ye the same thin', stranger."

Richard took in every aspect of the man. Through the open cape, he could see what looked like an old faded military uniform. With the war over, the roads of the country were overrun with former soldiers left with no funds and no employment. Had this one taken to the High Toby for his livelihood? Or was he just a traveler sheltering from the storm as well?

"The river is flooded and our carriage became stuck. We are waiting here until morning."

The stranger, taking note of the cultured accents of a gentleman, nodded his head. "Where be young Danny? I'm 'is cousin, John Wiggins, former private of His Majesty's army. Been livin' here since his ma died last spring."

Richard dropped his weapon to his side, certain it wouldn't have fired even had he needed it to. He frowned as the young man removed his dripping hat. "Do you often leave the boy alone like this?"

"I don't usually leave 'im, sir, but I been lookin' for work and got caught by the storm." John Wiggins had the same dark eyes and hair of his young cousin, but his face was leaner, with a scar across one cheek.

Angelica, who'd been sitting quietly throughout the encounter, rose on somewhat shaky knees. "Mr. Wiggins, I am Miss Markham and this is Lord Blackstone, and we are grateful for the use of your family's cottage. Please remove your wet coat and come near the fire."

The earl moved from the chair on which he'd been sitting, gesturing for young John to be seated. The man removed his coat to reveal a tattered uniform from which all the buttons were missing. He was rather a forlorn sight, which touched Angelica's heart.

As the earl engaged John in conversation about Danny and their life, it occurred to her that the former Private Wiggins might be able to help her get away from Richard come morning. As she raised her gaze to the earl, she felt a tightening in her chest. She wished she didn't have to flee from him, but he was as determined as ever to return her to Edenfield.

Regardless of her need to make plans, Angelica was too fatigued to think properly. She excused herself and went to the small alcove to lie on the bed fully clothed. For a long time she listened to the murmur of men's voices discussing Waterloo. The young soldier had been brave enough to face the French. Would he have the courage to help her escape from Lord Blackstone? She would find out in the morning.

Angelica awoke with a start. Silence reigned in the small cottage. She jumped up and peered around the curtain, but the room was empty, the open front door allowing the morning sun to fill the room. She wondered where everyone had gone. She retrieved her black traveling gown which had dried during the night and quickly changed. Then she set out to find Richard.

Going to the threshold, she covered her eyes to shade them from the brightness of the morning sun. As her vision adjusted to the light, she could see great pools of water around the cottage. She noted that two sets of footprints left the porch. One set included large and small ones headed in the direction that Danny had led the horses the night before. The other, large ones only, went off in the direction of their stranded carriage.

Certain that Richard had gone to the carriage while John and Danny saw to the horses, she followed the Wigginses' footprints knowing this was her best opportunity to get away, yet somehow feeling she was betraying Richard by leaving. Thinking that a foolish thought, she hurried to find John, hoping she could convince him to help her.

Within minutes she came to a large stone building which had seen better days. She could hear Danny chattering away to his older cousin. She stepped into the old structure, spying Richard's matched bays and a large animal that looked more suited to pulling a plow than carrying a soldier.

Danny was busy brushing one of the bays, while John was putting hay in each stall. Looking up, he spied Angelica and straightened, pulling his hat from his head. "Miss Markham."

"Mr. Wiggins, might I have a word with you?"

"Aye, ye can, but call me John, miss." The former soldier put down his pitchfork and walked to where the lady stood.

Angelica took a deep breath, then began. "John, I should like to hire you to take me to York, at once."

"Why, Miss Markham, I'd be pleased to 'elp ye out, but I'm afeared I can't. 'Is lordship done 'ired me. Wants me to come along to Blackstone Abbey with Danny in the next day or so."

Angelica at first was delighted that Richard had shown compassion for the young man and his cousin. But that reaction was quickly replaced with anger. *She* needed John; how dare the earl discover a conscience now!

"Are ye alright, miss?" John thought the lady looked a bit pale.

"No, John, I am not. But it seems there is little you can do to help, thanks to Lord Blackstone. It appears I shall have to walk to York." Saying that Angelica left the barn. With no particular destination in mind, she wandered into the nearby woods, her shoulders sagging in defeat. After walking for several minutes, she settled herself on a log, heedless of the dampness. She was overwhelmed with defeat. She had run out of ideas, and Edenfield was scarcely half a day's ride away.

Richard had risen early and gone to inspect the damage to his carriage. It was minimal, and all he required was someone to dig it out. In the light of day, he could see the bridge that they'd failed to reach the night before. The water had receded, and men with shovels worked at both ends, filling in the washed-out trenches cut by the raging river during the storm.

Thinking he might hire some of the men to dig out his curricle, he strolled to the bridge. He was speaking with a burly man, who seemed to be the leader, when a shout echoed from the opposite end of the bridge.

"Stand clear, you oafs. I'm in a hurry." The workmen scattered, and a carriage bearing two men bumped along the freshly laid dirt and rocks until it reached the smooth stone of the bridge.

Richard recognized an unshaven Viscount Edenfield, Angelica's stepbrother. His gaze moved to the short, husky man seated beside him. Instinctively he knew this was Lord

Paden. What the deuce was Giles thinking to be marrying Angel to a man who looked old as the ark and half as big?

As the carriage lumbered across the bridge, Giles spied Richard. The viscount reined his team to a halt and demanded, "Where the devil is my stepsister, Blackstone?"

Richard bowed to his neighbor, then allowed his gaze to drift to Giles's companion. Seeing the hostility on the lined face of Angel's so-called fiancé made the earl feel ill that she would soon belong to such a man. Without any conscious thought about what was best, he replied, "Dash it, man, can't you see my carriage is near ruin from being stuck in the mud? Do you think I have had time to run your caper-witted charge to ground, stranded like I am?"

The men in the carriage exchanged a look of relief and understanding. Giles was suddenly all affability. "Then I must thank you for your efforts and inform you that your assistance is no longer needed. Lord Paden, my stepsister's fiancé, and I are on our way to York, and we shall bring Miss Markham home."

Richard shrugged as if it didn't matter to him. "Very well, as you wish. I shall gladly return to my own affairs." The earl bowed, thinking his own affairs now included Miss Markham.

The viscount smugly tugged his hat, then whipped his team into a canter. Lord Paden gave Richard one last dismissive glance as the carriage disappeared down the road.

What the devil had gotten into him, Richard wondered. But he couldn't regret saving Angel from that aging roué. She was too beautiful to be forced into an unwanted marriage, no matter how advantageous. The problem was, he didn't have the least idea what he should do with her now.

Seeing the idle workman staring curiously, he pushed the problem from his mind and arranged to have his carriage dug out and returned to the Wigginses' cottage.

As he strolled back to tell Angel his change of heart, Richard realized the only place he could take her was to his mother in Bath. She would know what to do with the chit. He suddenly wondered if Angel would smile at him in that endearing way when he told her the news. The very thought made him pick up his pace.

Chapter Five

Richard halted at the open doorway and knew at once that the cottage was empty. In a flash, the disturbing thought that Angel had slipped away on foot to resume her journey to York filled him with unease. The very idea that she was so desperate to escape him caused an ache within him which he couldn't identify. In frustration, he turned and scanned the vista, then hurried down the path to where John and Danny were tending the horses.

Richard hoped Angel was at the old stable. He was overwhelmed with a sense of urgency to tell her that he was taking her to Bath instead of Edenfield.

Arriving at the stable, he called, "John, have you seen Miss Markham?"

The young man stepped out of a stall, pitchfork in hand. "Aye, my lord, she was 'ere a few minutes ago askin' bout me takin' 'er to York. If that's what ye want, I'll do it."

Richard smiled as relief filled him. "She'll change her mind about returning to York once I tell her my news. Where has she gotten to?"

"Wandered into the woods just there." John pointed out the direction.

"Some men from the village are bringing my curricle. If you will ready the carriage, Miss Markham and I shall leave as soon as I find her. We are going to Bath, but I shall return to Blackstone Abbey before you arrive."

"Very good, my lord." John beamed. "We'll be there."

Richard went in search of Angel. He soon came upon her perched on a fallen log, looking forlorn. "Good morning, my dear."

The lady started at the sound of his voice and a pair of violet-blue eyes gazed bleakly at him. "Good morning, my lord."

Coming to stand in front of her, Richard said, "I have just spoken with your brother."

Angelica bounded up, a hint of fear showing on her beautiful face. "He is here!"

Afraid she might rush into the woods before she heard the news, Richard took her by the shoulders. "He is on his way to York, even as we speak."

"But . . . how?"

"I was so overcome at the honor of meeting Lord Paden I simply forgot to mention that you were with me. Your stepbrother urged me to return home before he set out for York." The earl smiled as he dropped his hands from her and watched the dawning realization on Angel's face.

"Oh, Richard, you are wonderful!" Angelica threw her arms around his neck and, without a thought, kissed him. Suddenly realizing the impropriety of her actions she stepped back and blushed at the growing grin on Richard's handsome face.

Hoping to cover her confusion, she said, "So, you will take me to York?"

"Never, dear girl."

"But I thought since you . . ." Angelica's voice petered out. What was the earl planning on doing with her? Had he mistaken her kiss as an invitation to offer herself carte blanche? Straightening her shoulders, she haughtily asked, "What pray tell, are your plans, sir?"

Richard was amused at her tone. "Don't be cross as crabs with me. 'Tis only that York is out of the question. Would you have us overtake Giles on the road there, for I never knew a man who was more cow-handed handling the ribbons. I'm taking you to my mother in Bath."

Relief flooded Angelica. He might be a notorious rake, but he was still her old dear friend. "You truly are a knight to the rescue. I should like to go to Bath."

Richard entwined her arm with his. "What say you to breakfast in Throcking? This business of rescuing a damsel in distress leaves one rather sharp set."

Angelica laughed. She liked the feel of Richard's arm beneath her hand. Suddenly the future was again bright. She would stay with Lady Blackstone until she reached her majority. Then what?

Looking up at Richard as they made their way back to the Wigginses' cottage, Angelica knew she didn't want to think beyond the present. She would merely enjoy her time in Bath with the earl and his mother. A future without Richard suddenly looked dreary.

Augusta, Dowager Countess of Blackstone, resided in a comfortable house on Great Pulteney Street in Bath. Her decision to move from the family home had come a year earlier when, arriving unexpectedly at their town house in Berkeley Square, she'd come upon a party of her son and his raffish friends, each with an extremely vulgar actress in tow. She'd promptly turned on her heel and ordered the carriage to take her to her cousin in Bath, vowing not to set foot in any of her son's residences until he had a proper wife.

After staying with her cousin for six months, Augusta at last gave up waiting for her son to fall in with her plans and leased the house in which she currently lived with her outspoken sister, Mrs. Gertrude Harris. Though the dowager's sibling had inherited a comfortable income at the death of her husband, she'd been delighted to join Lady Blackstone in Bath.

On this warm August afternoon the ladies were seated in the drawing room, waiting for tea to be brought. Gertrude, red-haired with a smattering of freckles on her plump face, sat reading the Bath papers. She lowered the news and inquired, "Do you wish to go to the theater this week, Augusta? The newspaper states they are doing a revival of Sheridan's *The Rivals*."

The dowager, a handsome woman who'd grown stout and grey with age, looked up from her book of poetry, thoughtfully tugging at the lappet on her frilly white cap. "Perhaps on Friday, my dear."

The door to the drawing room opened at that moment and Bergman, the butler, entered. "My lady, Lord Blackstone and a young lady are here."

Hope swelled in Augusta's heart as she sat up. While Richard had visited her regularly, he'd brought no one with him before. "Show them in quickly, Bergman."

Within minutes Richard and a young lady dressed in the black of mourning entered the room, crushing Augusta's plans for a possible marriage for her son. She eyed the woman closely, thinking something was familiar about her.

Richard surveyed his mother to gauge her mood. He was pleased to see her smiling. Looking back at Angel encouragingly, he thought her very pale in her black traveling dress and bonnet, her eyes looking more violet than blue. He fought the urge to take her in his arms to reassure her, for he suddenly realized that her welfare had begun to occupy his thoughts constantly. Turning to the seated ladies, he said, "Good afternoon, Mother, Aunt Gertrude."

The dowager arched one brow. "What a surprise, my dear. I thought you were off to some house party in the country." She leaned a mildly lined cheek up for her son to kiss.

"I had an unexpected change of plans."

Gertrude Harris eyed the beauty in black with hostility. Her opinion of her nephew's lifestyle couldn't be lower and she always let him know it. "Richard, this is a new low for you. Always before you allowed the gentleman to get cold in the ground before making off with the widow."

Richard opened his mouth as if to give his aunt a tongue-lashing, but he knew he'd be wasting his breath. His concern was getting Angel settled, and his aunt's comment had left the young lady with pink cheeks. He smiled reassuringly at her, ignoring Gertrude's jibe.

The dowager was stunned at Richard's acceptance of the barb, for he usually returned his aunt's rude remarks with equal sharpness.

"Mother, you remember Miss Angelica Markham from Edenfield. Angel, my mother, Lady Blackstone, and my aunt, Mrs. Gertrude Harris."

As the young lady made a proper curtsy to them, Augusta stared at the girl in black mourning garb. Good heavens, this beauty couldn't be that skinny child Richard used to bring home for tea, but it appeared so. "Why, my dear Angel, I wouldn't have recognized you. You've changed so. Forgive me, I'm forgetting my manners. Please accept my condolences on your loss."

Angelica was pleased that the countess called her by her childhood name, but was surprised to find herself so embarrassed by the situation. "Oh, I am not in mourning, Lady Blackstone. This is . . ." She trailed off and looked at Richard.

The earl, realizing how difficult explaining would be, took Angelica's hand. "Mother, 'tis a long story, and Angel is fatigued. We were hoping she might stay here with you. I'm sure once you've heard her story you will agree, but for now I think the lady needs to rest."

Augusta was curious, but the one thing she took note of was Richard's gaze as it rested on Angel. The look was almost a caress. Was it possible her son was enamored with their beautiful neighbor?

Pulling herself from this hopeful thought, the dowager smiled at her guest. "I should be delighted for you to stay, my dear. Gertrude, pray, have one of the maids take Miss Markham to the Blue Room, and speak with Cook about two more places for dinner."

Gertrude, filled with curiosity about the mysterious young lady they called Angel, escorted the girl from the room, hoping Augusta would find out why Richard was in company with a genteel young lady. She often criticized him for his more outrageous exploits because they occasionally embarrassed her sister, but he always kept to women of a certain type, and the lady he'd arrived with was definitely not such a woman.

Augusta waited until her sister had led Miss Markham from the room. She gestured for her son to take the seat across from her. "Richard, I am certain I don't have to remind you of the danger to Angel's reputation to be traveling alone with you, so I shall simply ask why the young lady needs to stay with me."

Richard quickly told his mother the tale. When he came to the part about meeting the baron at the bridge, the earl became so agitated that he stood and began to pace. The more he spoke of protecting Angel from the unwanted marriage, the more Augusta was certain her son had fallen in love with the beauty and didn't even realize it.

Settling back into his chair when he'd finished, Richard grew quiet and then said, "Mother, we have traveled alone for two days together. I think I should do the proper thing and marry her."

It took every bit of strength Augusta had to prevent her from shouting yes, but she wanted her son's marriage to be a happy one. He must come to realize his true feeling and not offer for the girl out of duty.

"You know Angel better than I. Do you think she would accept a marriage of convenience?"

"No, I don't."

"Then I think it best not to worry her over that matter. Leave her with me. I am certain you have much to do at the estate since your visit was interrupted. I shall need some time to dress the dear girl before I introduce her to Bath society."

Richard frowned. "You intend to take her about?"

"But of course, my dear. Angel needs a husband of her choosing. Besides, I shall enjoy outfitting her and escorting her to the private parties of my friends."

The earl grew quiet. He was certain Angel would be considered a diamond of the first water in Bath. But he was equally certain he didn't want to be around to watch all the gentleman swarm about her. The very thought caused a sharp pain in his chest. What was the matter with him? It was high time he got back to his own affairs. All he needed was the charms of some lusty actress or some sultry widow to help him forget about the dark-haired beauty upstairs.

Richard rose abruptly and kissed his mother. "I think I shall allow you to handle matters for Angel. If I leave now I can reach Blackstone Abbey before midnight."

Augusta suppressed a smile as she watched her son's retreating back. "Do come again soon, I am certain Angel will wish to thank you and introduce you to her choice of a husband."

The drawing-room door slammed shut. The dowager chuckled. He would be back, and sooner than he realized.

Later that evening, Augusta watched Angel struggle to hide her disappointment at the news that his lordship had returned home quite suddenly. The dowager was certain the pair were in love. Now all she had to do was make certain that Angelica didn't attract some eligible gentleman until her son came to his senses.

Two days later Richard found himself strolling down Haymarket Street toward the King's Theatre in the hope of finding some new actress to tease him out of his dark mood. He'd returned to the abbey, only to find he couldn't concentrate. Even his tenants had praised Angel for her kindness in helping with the sick. In desperation, he'd packed and returned to Town.

Now going round to the stage door, which was propped opened due to the heat, he recognized several of the women milling around backstage while the sounds of someone rehearsing onstage echoed out the door.

Stepping into the theatre, Richard halted as a tall, buxom blonde with a painted face and dressed as a shepherdess came to hang on his arm. Her stage name was Lilac Windemere.

"Why, if it ain't Lord Blackstone! Did you get bored with the girls what went to Lord Yardley's little party?" The actress pressed herself close to the earl. "Never had a gentleman get bored with me."

Lilac suddenly leaned over and kissed her prey.

Richard choked at the smell of cheap perfume, and he wanted to push the woman away. When she drew back and smiled, he was filled with memories of the sweet innocence of Angel's kiss in the woods. His gaze swept the actresses who watched Lilac's attempts to snare a benefactor. These women weren't what he desired any longer.

With a bow and a tip of his hat, Richard said, "Ladies, I have an appointment in Bath." He turned and left, certain of what he wanted.

Angelica plucked a red rose from the trellis, then wandered to the marble bench at the back of the small garden at Lady Blackstone's house in Bath. Dressed in a new pink sprig muslin day gown with white lace at the sleeves, her black hair now fashionably arranged, she settled in the shade, wondering where Richard was at this moment. When the countess had told her he'd gone without so much as saying goodbye, Angelica's heart felt as if it were crushed. She knew she'd made the dreadful mistake of falling in love with her old friend.

When Angelica had come downstairs the following morning, Lady Blackstone had insisted on a new wardrobe for her guest and had announced that she'd called in a seamstress. She'd spoken of the parties and other entertainments they would attend in Bath, but all Angelica could think of was Richard and where he was at that moment.

Angelica plucked a velvety petal from the rose she held and sniffed its sweet scent. It would be a long month and a half before she received her inheritance and could find living quarters of her own. What if Richard returned before then? Could she keep from revealing her feelings to the man she loved? He was so anxious to get back to his rakish life, he'd left without bidding her farewell. He'd never given her a second thought.

The crunch of gravel on the garden path alerted Angelica that someone was joining her. She quickly swiped at a tear that streamed down her cheek and looked up; then her breath caught in her throat. The earl strode toward her looking rakishly handsome in a blue coat with grey pantaloons. His blond hair glistened in the afternoon sun.

Angelica rose on shaking knees. Her heart began to race as she took in the tender look in his amber eyes. Dare she hope? "R-Richard, this is a surprise. I didn't expect to see you again so soon. What brings you back to Bath?"

"A lady, my dear."

Angelica's heart plummeted. He'd found some new dalliance. Afraid she might cry, she nodded and looked away, fingering the small roses on the trellis, then bitterly said, "I am sure she will be delighted to be the object of your desire."

"She doesn't appear to be."

Richard watched as Angel spun around in surprise, her lips trembling. He stepped closer and slid his arms around her waist, drawing her to him. "Are you delighted to be the object of my desire?"

Angel, unable to speak, smiled up at him, and her eyes brimmed with unshed tears. Her dark curls bounced as she nodded her head vigorously.

"It is truly more than mere desire, my love, for you are the lady who stole my heart." Richard's mouth closed over Angelica's, and this time the lady surrendered with a sigh of pleasure.

After several passion-filled moments, the earl drew back and said, "I love you, my dear. Will you marry me?"

"Oh, Richard, are you sure you can give up all the . . . others."

Tightening his arms around her waist, Richard grinned. "I've already forsaken that way of life, all I want is you, my very own Angel."

"I do so love you, my very own Rake." Angelica again surrendered to the pleasure of Richard's kiss.

From the upstairs window, the dowager and her sister briefly watched the scene in the garden; then, feeling they were intruding, they left the lovers to their joy.

As they went down to tea, perhaps because she had not thought of it sooner, Augusta complained, "I should have known it would take an angel to reform a rake."

THE NOTORIOUS
NOBLEMAN

Nancy Lawrence

Gavin Northcote, Duke of Warminster, had just reached the outermost boundaries of his Sussex estate when he chanced a look at the late-afternoon sky and saw the green-grey clouds of a thunderstorm forming overhead. The clouds were low and heavy with rain, and he knew in an instant he wouldn't be able to outrun the deluge. He had been galloping like a hellion for miles, and his horse was nearly spent. He knew himself to be faring no better.

His head was throbbing, and his arm felt as if it were on fire. He had been riding since he'd left London early that morning, so his backside hurt. His temper was frayed and his nerves were on edge; he cursed the luck that had already failed him once that day—the same luck that now showed every promise of failing him once again.

He topped a hill just as he saw the first flash of lightning in the distance. His horse snorted and caricoled in warning, and he gave the animal's neck a gentle pat. "I know, boy. I know."

From the vantage of the hilltop, he could discern the roofline of a small cottage partially hidden by trees in the dell below. He made for it, sending his horse flying down the gently sloping terrain with a speed and recklessness he would have found invigorating under any other circumstance. Now all he could think of was the amount of precious time he would lose by having to wait out the storm—time that could be better spent putting as much distance as possible between himself and London—and the havoc he had wrought there.

He reached the cottage just as a drop of rain splattered against his cheek. Along the back of the dwelling had been erected a small lean-to, and he led his horse to it. He had just finished tethering the animal beneath the shelter of the shed when a low rumble of thunder sounded and the rain began to fall in earnest.

Gavin made his way around the cottage as quickly as his stiff and weary legs could carry him. A flash of light warned him to expect yet another crack of thunder, so he pushed at the cottage door. It didn't give.

Cursing, his patience at an end, he threw his considerable weight against the door, sending it crashing back on its hinges at the same moment a low roll of thunder rumbled across the roof of the fragile little cottage. He stepped inside and slammed the door shut against the weather with the same force he had used to open it. This time he heard the wood of the door splinter.

The cottage was nothing more than a single room with one small window to allow in the daylight, but with the storm clouds blocking out the sun, the place was dim and shadowed and uninviting. He grumbled yet another curse and gave himself a slight shake, sending droplets of rain scattering across the floor. Sweeping his dripping hat from his head, he tossed it negligently onto a small table set beneath the window and immediately heard a distinct gasp come from the shadows in the far corner of the room.

Suddenly alert, he willed his eyes to penetrate the darkness of that corner. At first, he couldn't see anything, but instinct told him he wasn't alone, that someone else was there with him. Then he saw her.

In the shadows he could just distinguish a woman's face. Against the darkness of the cottage, her complexion contrasted very well, for she was quite pale from shock and her eyes were wide as saucers as she stared, unblinking, back at him.

He relaxed slightly. She was no threat; in fact, she appeared even more startled to see him than he was to see her.

"That's a hell of a storm," he said, as he gingerly pulled his gloves from his hands and tossed them onto the table. But when he unbuttoned the front of his coat and began to slowly shrug out of it, he heard her gasp again.

He looked over at her then, realizing for the first time that she hadn't spoken or moved. "What in the name of hell is the matter with you?" he demanded.

The woman stared back at him a moment. "Why—why are you taking off your coat?" she asked in a voice that was little more than a croak.

"Because it happens to be wet."

"Y-you won't remove anything else, will you?"

He let loose a derisive grunt. "Not for the time being, so you need not behave quite so theatrically!"

That taunt banished the last of the fear from her expression. "Theatrically? May I remind you that it was you who startled *me*? There was really no need to have broken the door down, you know!"

He draped his coat over one of the two chairs at the table and said, in a weary tone, "It was jammed shut."

"*I* was able to get it open easily enough."

There was no mistaking the challenge in her tone, but the duke chose to ignore it. He pulled the only other chair away from the table and sank slowly down onto it, wincing slightly as he did so.

The young woman trained a wary gaze upon him and asked, rather tentatively, "Do you suppose anyone else might be out in the storm? Do you think anyone else will seek shelter here?"

"If you're asking if there is another person alive as foolish as we to be out in weather like this, the answer must certainly be no."

She stiffened slightly. "I'm not foolish. I'm just not very adept at reading the skies and judging the weather."

He allowed his gaze to rake over her in a manner calculated to dampen any further conversation. "You are very foolish," he pronounced. "But then, so am I."

The woman left the shadows to step farther into the room. Her tone had a natural dignity as she said, "You needn't be insulting. If we are to remain together until the storm is over, we should at least be civil to one another."

He flicked a disdainful glance in her direction. "*Should* we?"

Now quite determined, the woman cast him a smile he immediately recognized as one customarily worn by society's best hostesses.

"Of course! I don't imagine we need stand on ceremony," she said. "Perhaps we should introduce ourselves? I am Lady Julia Pettingale." She waited, and when he didn't answer, she prompted, "And you are . . . ?"

For the first time since he'd entered the cottage, Gavin took a good look at her, letting his dark eyes sweep over her, covering every visible inch of her body in a slow, deliberate manner.

He looked at her not once but twice, and almost groaned out loud. She was right, he realized. They *were* going to have to wait out the storm together; and, dammit, she wasn't even pretty.

Oh, she seemed passable-looking, with large eyes of a color he couldn't distinguish in the shadows of the cottage. She was young—no more than five-and-twenty summers, he thought, and she had a straight nose and a soft, full mouth. The fit of her emerald green riding habit told him that her figure was good. She was deep bosomed and slim hipped; he usually liked his women that way. Still, if the dim light of the room could be trusted, he could see that beneath her stylish tricorn hat, she was a redhead.

Once again he silently cursed the luck that had already failed him twice that day. If he had to be marooned in an abandoned hut with a woman, did she have to have red hair? She might as well have had a horn growing out of her forehead for all the attraction he felt toward her.

He resigned himself to his fate. He said simply, "Warminster."

"Warminster?" she repeated. She took a step toward him and asked with interest, "Are you the Duke of Warminster?"

"Yes. Do I know you?"

"Oh, no!" she said, and she laughed slightly. "You don't know me, but I believe I know of you. *You're* the man everyone whispers about."

He shot one dark brow skyward. "You're very blunt!"

"I see no reason to speak other than the truth," she answered reasonably.

"Is that so? Then allow me to be equally truthful and tell you that you are trespassing on my land!"

"No, am I? Goodness, I must have gone farther abroad than I thought. I didn't realize I had strayed so far from the vicarage."

He looked at her darkly. "The *vicarage*? Don't tell me you *live* there!"

"No, but my best friend, Harriet Clouster, does. She's married to the vicar, and I've come to visit for a few weeks."

The irony was almost too much for him. Had he been stuck in a rainstorm with any other woman, he wouldn't have cared. A wench from the village, a tart from the back slums of London's Bear Alley—with one of them he could have found a most agreeable way in which to wait out the storm.

But instead he was stuck with a redhead. A redhead who

was a prim-and-proper, well-born lady. A redhead who had taken up residence at the vicarage.

If he'd been a religious man, he would have thought God was trying to punish him for what he had done earlier that morning—and that He had found a good way to do it.

"You're miles from the vicarage," he said. "How the devil did you get here?"

"I was riding. I guess I wasn't paying attention to where I was going or how far afield I had gone."

He shot her a dark look of disbelief. "If you were out riding, where's your horse?"

"Why, he is just outside."

"You are mistaken. There was no sign of a horse when I arrived here."

Julia Pettingale uttered a small, incoherent protest and went to the window. "I assure you, I was riding a horse. I left him right there, outside the cottage."

"Did you tether him?"

"Well, no, I-I didn't," she said, rather defensively. "The storm came up so fast and . . . and I suppose I was thinking only of getting into shelter."

"Didn't you know there was a shed propped up against the back of this hut?"

"No, I didn't. Is that where you put your horse?"

He nodded, causing a shard of pain to travel up his arm to his shoulder.

Julia watched him a moment, then looked from his drawn face to the window. "Do you think my horse will be safe out there? Perhaps you should go out and find him?"

"Go out and . . . ! No, young lady, I shall *not* go out and find your horse. In case you haven't looked outside—"

"You don't suppose he'll be struck by lightning, do you?" she asked, interrupting him before his tirade could be fully launched.

He didn't think it would be such a bad thing for the horse

if it were. Judging from the looks of its oh-so-respectable mistress, the beast was probably nothing more than a sedate nag such as ladies of breeding rode in Hyde Park. He rather suspected that if he were a horse, he'd rather suffer a lightning bolt between the eyes than have to live the life of a Rotten Row hack.

Almost he considered saying so to Lady Julia Pettingale, but there was something about her eyes, gone wide with concern, and the manner in which she caught her full lower lip between her even, white teeth that conjured a long-forgotten emotion. The biting retort that had been poised on the tip of his tongue died away, and he said, grudgingly, "I shouldn't worry about your horse. He's probably back at the vicarage by now. Animals have a way of fending for themselves."

"I suppose you are right," she said, but she still looked doubtful. She stood watching the Duke, hoping for more conversation to help take her mind off the storm and off the possible fate of her horse, but he offered none.

As Julia's eyes swept over him, she noticed that he wore no cravat and his shirt was open at his throat, allowing her a teasing glimpse of the dark curls that crept up toward his neck from the broad expanse of his chest. His hair was dark, with a natural curl where it lay at the back of his neck and over his ears. His eyes were dark, too, and he appeared to be a good ten years older than she.

He also appeared to be not the least interested in conversation. His mouth was set in a grim line and there was a harsh, rather ruthless expression about his eyes that Julia had never before seen on a man; she wondered over it.

And then she saw him shudder slightly.

At first she thought she had been mistaken, that her eyes had played a trick on her in the dim light of the cottage, but he did it again. It was only a slight tremor—the merest of movements—but she saw it.

Another rip of lightning lit the sky and flashed through the window, and Julia suddenly saw the cause of his shivers.

There was a large, dark spot on the left sleeve of his brown coat. It was fresh and still damp.

"You're hurt!" she exclaimed. Her expressive eyes traveled from the growing stain on his sleeve up to his face. "That's blood, isn't it?"

"It's nothing," he muttered, tightly.

"But you need attention! At the very least, you should have a physician!"

"I don't need a physician," he said, shooting her a forbidding look; then he leaned his head back to rest it against the wall, closing his eyes, dismissing her.

He hoped she would take the hint and leave him alone; he hoped the sudden stillness in the room meant she had retreated to that shadowed corner to wait out the rest of the storm in silence, but after a moment, he heard her begin to move about the cottage.

He did his best to block out every sound she made, but instead, even the merest noise seemed to be magnified. He heard her rattle about in a small cupboard, then open and shut the cottage door. He muttered a strangled curse, knowing full well that if she didn't keep still, in a matter of mere seconds he was probably going to do or say something that he would no doubt regret.

But no sooner had he formed that notion than her movements came to a sudden and complete stop. Curiosity caused him to open his eyes.

While the duke had been wishing her in Jericho, Julia Pettingale had lit the fire in the hearth. She had also lit a tallow candle. He watched her set it down on the table beside him, along with a sheet of bed linen and a bottle of brown liquid. The stuff looked very much like a bourbon of some sort, and his opinion of her immediately rose a notch or two.

Dropping to her knees in front of him, Julia said briskly, "Take off your coat."

He looked at her with fire in his eye. "No, I won't take off my coat, but I will take that bottle."

She was there before him, snatching up the bottle and moving it out of his reach. "Take off your coat so I may examine your arm."

"I'll see myself in hell first! If you think for one minute I'm going to allow you to play the ministering angel—!"

"Don't argue with me," she said, cutting him off with an air of assurance that silenced him, "and don't deceive yourself. I am not a ministering angel. You may believe me when I say that I do not at all care if you should live or die."

"Then leave me alone!" he commanded, and with his good arm he caught her wrist just as she reached up to grasp the lapel of his riding jacket.

Julia tried to pull away, but he held her fast. "You're going to bleed to death if you don't let me do something about your arm," she said in a slow, measured tone.

"You said yourself, you didn't care if I should live or die," he countered.

Julia cocked her head to one side and looked up at him, the hint of a rather charming smile pulling at her lips. "I lied."

He hadn't expected her to reply so, and for a moment he was a little startled. Julia Pettingale was still kneeling before him, her slim wrist still captured in his hand. She had taken off the riding gloves she had been wearing, and the little tricorn hat was gone, too, removing any last remaining doubts he might have had about her coloring.

Yes, she was a redhead, but she wasn't a redhead of the typical fashion. In the light of the tallow candle he saw that her hair was more of a dark auburn and it was arranged very flatteringly about her face. She didn't have a typical redhead's complexion, either. Her skin was smooth and white, and there was no sign of those ghastly freckles that were the bane of a redhead's existence. The green of her riding habit matched the green of her eyes. She gazed back up at him with a look of calm purpose.

"Please take off your coat," she said again. "I will help you."

"I don't need your help," he said, ungraciously, as he released his hold of her. "I just need that bottle."

"You may have a drink from it, but you may not have the entire bottle."

"Why not?"

"I might have to use some of the spirits to clean your wound. But I cannot know that until you take off your coat."

He cast her one last malevolent look, then silently leaned slightly forward and began to shrug his arms out of his sleeves.

Julia didn't try to help him. A duke he may be, she thought, but he has no grace and fewer manners. Even now, as he shifted his weight to work his arms out of his coat, he scuffled his feet slightly and one muddy boot left a footprint where the skirt of her riding habit had billowed out on the floor. Julia yanked the precious velvet skirt out from under his feet, but it was too late; the damage had been done. He muttered something, but she thought it sounded more like a curse than an apology; and when he leaned a bit closer to her, she could smell the odor of old spirits on his breath.

Her husband, when he was alive, had smelled the same way; of brandy and tobacco and, sometimes, of women's perfume. An old, forgotten feeling of disgust swept over her as she realized that the duke appeared to be the kind of man she most disliked—the kind of man who valued horses and sport and drink above all else, the kind of man her husband had been.

Gavin gave one final, thorough curse as he tugged his wounded arm from his coat, and Julia saw that his entire shirtsleeve was covered with blood. Over this sleeve, a wad of cloth had been pressed against the wound and inexpertly tied in place with a length of material that had probably once been a most immaculate cravat.

"You bandaged this yourself, didn't you?" she asked, studying the makeshift dressing. When he didn't answer, she poured a small amount of bourbon into a chipped teacup and handed it to him. "Drink this."

He didn't need to be asked a second time. He threw back the bourbon in one swift motion and held the cup out for more.

"I cannot like the thought of speeding a man toward inebriation," Julia said, casting him a doubtful look, "but I suppose you shall need something to lessen the pain."

He lifted one dark brow. "Worried? Afraid too much bourbon might make me behave as less than a gentleman?"

"I believe you have already proved yourself to be less than gentlemanly."

"A few rude words—is that your idea of ungentleman-like behavior? You *are* a prim little thing!"

A rush of angry heat covered Julia's cheeks, but she decided it best not to answer his taunts. Instead, she refilled the cup and handed it to him, watching as again he downed its contents in a single swallow.

The next time he thrust the chipped cup at her, she took it from him and put it down on the table; then she set about carefully untying the cloth on his arm. When she slowly lifted away one corner of the bandage, he winced.

"I'm sorry. I shall try not to hurt you."

"You didn't," he retorted, but the white lines about his mouth told her otherwise.

She stood up, relieved by the chance to put some distance between them. "I've set a bowl outside to catch some rainwater. I'll use it to cleanse the wound. But first, you shall need to take your shirt off, too."

She didn't wait for him to reply, but went to the door and darted out into the storm to fetch the full bowl of water. By the time she turned back into the room, he had shrugged out of his shirt.

Julia pushed a rain-soaked strand of hair back from her

forehead and tried to keep her attention focused on his wounded arm. Too often, though, she found her gaze straying toward the mat of curly black hair sprinkled across his chest and to the breadth of his shoulders. There were small scars along his chest and across the solid ridges of his belly. One large scar stretched along the top of one shoulder, as if he had once broken his collarbone and it had healed improperly. She didn't doubt for a moment he had got those scars from fights. He was a big man; a man of brawn, who, according to rumor, used his size and strength to his advantage in all things.

But his strength was quickly deserting him. The effort of taking his shirt off had cost him; his face had gone pale and his expression was grim. Julia silently refilled the teacup and handed it to him, then turned her attention toward his wound.

With a piece of the clean bedsheet she had found, she began to gingerly bathe his arm in rainwater. When she had washed away a good portion of the blood, she saw that the wound was clean and not too deep, with no jagged edges. She had seen that kind of wound before. It was the kind only a sword produced.

"You received this in a duel, didn't you?" she asked. She had resolved to keep any emotion from her voice, but her tone had sounded accusing, even to her own ears.

"What do you know about duels?"

"I know they are against the law."

"Laws are for cattle," he said through clenched teeth. "I never let them dictate my behavior."

"And only see where it has got you."

His dark eyes widened slightly as his gaze flicked over her. "You argue like a woman."

"And you argue like William."

He frowned. "Who the devil is William?"

"My husband. He's dead now. But when he was alive he, too, caroused and fought and drank too much."

"He was probably driven to it," muttered the duke,

then he sucked his breath in sharply as Julia unconsciously applied a bit too much pressure on his arm.

She rocked back on her heels and fixed him with an icy glare. "You," she pronounced with heartfelt sincerity, "are a horrid man!"

"So I have been told," he answered, unperturbed.

"Do you not care that I think you are horrid?"

"Not at all."

"What if I were to tell you that I think you quite odious?"

"I should never concern myself with anything so trifling."

"You should, for your behavior is a source of great gossip. That is why everyone whispers about you. I dare say your reputation is vile, indeed!"

"People shall think what they like about me, no matter what I do," he replied curtly.

Julia cast him a speculative glance. "Ever since I arrived at the vicarage, I have heard bits of stories about you and your reputation." She chanced a look up at him and found that he was watching her, quite unmoved, his expression unreadable. Encouraged, she said, "My friend, Harriet, whispers about you to her friends, but she won't tell me anything about you. I can only conclude, then, that you are quite scandalous."

"Indeed?" he asked blandly. "Are you asking me to confirm whether or not your conclusion is true?"

"If you would be so good," she answered dulcetly. "To own the truth, I've never before met anyone who was truly rakish and depraved."

He scowled at her. "And what makes you think you would recognize such behavior if you saw it?"

"I recognized it enough to know it is probably how you came by your arm. You fought a duel this morning, and I should hazard to wager you fought it over a lady." When he didn't answer, she looked up at him and said, "Well, *didn't* you?"

"You would lose the wager," he retorted, unwilling to discuss the subject.

"Did you fight over a game of cards, then?"

"Not this time."

She turned her attention back to his arm and quietly worked over his wound. After a moment, she couldn't resist asking, "I don't suppose you would care to tell me *why* you fought a duel today?"

"No, I would not," he said curtly. "And I should advise you not to pry into areas of which you know nothing."

She poured some more bourbon into the teacup for him and said softly, "I know that it takes two men to fight a duel. What happened to the other man?"

He looked at her over the rim of the cup. "I don't know," he said quite honestly.

"Is he . . . ? Is he . . . ?" She couldn't bring herself to finish the question because she suddenly wasn't sure she wanted to know the answer. She hated to think she was bandaging the arm of a man who had killed someone only hours before.

Gavin saw the distress reflected in her eyes. "You're very concerned over a situation of which you know precious little," he said, dampeningly. "Save your pity! The man I fought this morning received no more than he deserved."

"Did he deserve to die? Or did he just deserve to be wounded?"

"I told you, I don't know his condition. When I left him, he was still alive and under the care of his second."

Julia wished he had said something else. She wished he had reassured her that the man he had fought was alive and well and suffered from nothing more than a flesh wound. She wished he had told her anything—even lies— as long as he had told her that he hadn't hurt anyone; for she was suddenly most heartily convinced the duke had killed the man with whom he had fought the duel.

Of a sudden, Julia couldn't bring herself to touch him, and she sat back on her heels, unable to trust her trembling hands and equally unable to meet his eyes. Lord Warminster was, of all things, the kind of man she most disliked, and now she was filled with a sudden dread that his conduct was not only unscrupulous but criminal.

After a long moment she looked up at him and saw that his dark gaze had never wavered from her face. His look was watchful and knowing, and lacking any hint of repentance. Small wonder, then, that tales of his black conduct should circulate about the neighborhood, making him seem larger than life and as evil as the devil himself.

She forced herself to meet his dark eyes and asked, "Have you any way of discovering the man's condition?"

"I can think of nothing that would interest me less."

"Don't you care at all that you might have killed him?"

"Not in the least." He was quiet a moment; then he said in a grudging, yet gentler voice, "As it happens, my own second remained behind in London. He is a close and trusted friend, and he will come to me as soon as he has word of the man's fate."

"Then will you share the news with me when you've heard it?"

"Share it with . . . ! My dear young woman, what possible reason could you have for wanting to know that?"

"Please?" she persisted.

He scowled at her. "I never make promises."

A shiver of cold went through Julia, and she tried to dispel it by forcing herself to concentrate on his wound. She studied it a moment and said, "About your arm. It is not as bad as I originally thought, and I can bandage it up again, but I think it shall need to be sewn. You'll need a surgeon for that."

"I don't need a surgeon."

"Oh, but you do. The wound is much too—"

"And I don't need your advice!"

She pursed her lips together for a moment, then said, in an even tone, "I am merely trying to be a helpful, Christian woman."

He corrected her. "On the contrary. You're trying to be a managing and meddling woman."

Julia looked up at him quickly, an odd light of recognition in her green eyes. "Do you know, my husband used to say the very same thing."

"My sympathies to your husband."

Julia almost replied in anger, almost lost her temper and explained to this insufferable man what she thought of his manners. Instead she pursed her soft, full lips into a tight line before saying, still quite angry, "I'm going to wash your wound with the spirits now."

She didn't give him time to brace himself or argue. Instead, she swiftly doused bourbon on the cloth she had been using and pressed it against his arm.

Gavin sucked in his breath; then, just as quickly, he let out a stream of epithets that sent the color flying to her cheeks.

"You did that on purpose!" he accused, as soon as he could catch his breath.

She faced him with the calm of one who has tasted revenge. "You're being ridiculous. The wound has to be cleansed. You don't want to lose the use of your arm to infection, do you?"

A bitter string of curses rose in the back of his throat, but he checked them and concentrated instead on regaining mastery of himself.

He watched her douse the cloth with bourbon again, and he buttressed his will against what he knew was coming. This time, he wouldn't cry out; this time, he wouldn't let her surprise him into betraying an emotion as cheap as pain. This time, he'd show the prim-and-proper little widow who she was dealing with.

Julia worked over his wound, knowing all the while that he had steeled himself against her touch. She felt his dark eyes upon her, and she was a little unnerved by it.

"Talk to me," he commanded, after a moment in which he had clenched his teeth so tight his jaw hurt.

She looked up at him, her green eyes wide. "About what?"

"Anything! Talk about your husband—your William." His arm hurt like the devil, but he forced himself to concentrate instead on her. "Tell me about him. You still mourn, do you not? How long has it been?"

She decided to ignore his first question. "He's been gone these twelve months now. I'm just out of black ribbands."

His gaze swept over the form-fitting habit she wore. "From the way you are dressed, you look more like a merry widow than a grieving one."

Julia looked down at the green velvet material of her riding kit, then looked up to flash him a brilliant smile. "Thank you!"

"I didn't mean that as a compliment," he said, in a grumbling tone.

"Oh, but you were much more complimentary than you shall ever know. You see, my riding habit is my most prized possession."

That surprised a bark of laughter out of him. "Is it? Then I should wager your possessions are few, indeed!"

"Then I dare say you would win that wager," she replied, quite unperturbed. "I have, truly, nothing else of value."

His gaze swept over her again. With a practiced eye Gavin recognized the fine tailoring of the green velvet riding outfit she wore. The material was lush and full, and had probably been quite expensive at the time of its purchase. The jacket and skirt had been cut to accentuate the perfection of her figure. Workmanship like that didn't come cheap; yet he also realized that the style of the kit had to be at least five or six years old.

"I'm not certain I believe you," he said quite frankly. "You strike me as the kind of woman who would have new gowns, including new riding habits, every year. Why do you go on without them?"

"I go on without them because I have no choice to do

otherwise," she replied calmly. "I have no money, you see."

He said, dismissively, "I am told it is not uncommon for women to fall on hard times once they find themselves widowed."

"Is it? Then I shall take comfort in knowing I am not alone in my present circumstance," she said, with the hint of a smile that intrigued him. "It makes no never mind, for I don't intend to dwell on what has occurred in the past. Now that I've thrown off my black, I intend to don my old gowns and attend all the parties, all the balls and assemblies I am able. My stay with Harriet Clouster is my first social visit in more than a year, and I hope I may have many more."

He frowned. "Who the devil is Harriet Clouster?"

"I've already told you," she said with exaggerated patience. "Harriet Clouster is the vicar's wife. She is my oldest and dearest friend. We have known each other since our cradle days."

There was something in her tone that stung him. "You say that as if you expected me to know her."

"Well, she *is* the wife of your vicar, after all. Her husband has his living from you."

"Oh. *Him.*"

She almost laughed. "I don't suppose you and the vicar have very much in common."

"What in the name of hell do you mean by that?" he demanded, one dark brow flying to a challenging angle.

She didn't answer right away, but a moment later, she asked, in a quiet voice, "Do you always curse so in the presence of a lady?"

"No, dammit, I do not!" The words, from habit, were out before he could stop them, and he saw her full lips press into a tight line. He thought of apologizing, but discarded the notion as soon as it was born. He said instead, "It happens that I am rarely in a lady's presence."

"So it would seem," she murmured, vividly conjuring

the memory of all the many bits of conversation she had overheard about the duke's scandalous behavior.

"So! You *have* heard the rumors! What have you been told about me?"

She took up a clean piece of bed linen and began tearing long strips from its length. She said, evasively, "I don't think it wise for me to repeat tales I should never have overheard in the first place."

"Fainteheart!" he accused. "I would have pegged you as a woman with more bottom!"

"Oh, no!" she said with a slight laugh. "You shan't bully me into repeating nonsense!"

"Does that mean you don't believe any of the stories people whisper about me?"

"No. It means I believe only the *worst* of the stories!" she answered, with a smile of great sweetness.

Despite his resolution, the duke found himself smiling back, but he quickly schooled his expression into a frown and grumbled, "You're no different than all the others."

"In what manner?"

"You believe every wretched rumor and every vile story that passes from one clucking tongue to another."

"Do I?" she asked, with a credible imitation of wonder.

"Don't be coy, madam. It doesn't suit you!"

She ignored that stricture and said in a very businesslike tone, "Lift your arm, please."

He complied without thinking and watched as Julia pressed a pad of clean cloth against his wound and began to twine a strip of bed linen about his arm to hold it in place.

"If you truly believe I am as depraved as people say, you should never have stayed here with me," he said. "You should have left as soon as you discovered my identity. Common sense should have told you the danger you were in by remaining in my presence."

"And step instead out into a thunderstorm where I might be struck by lightning? Thank you, but I should rather remain here with you. You are the lesser of two evils, you see!"

"If anyone were to discover our situation, you would be quite ruined, you know."

"Why?" she asked most innocently. "*Should* I be afraid of you? *Are* you very evil?"

"Decidedly!"

"I don't believe it," she said with a slight shake of her head. "You don't strike me as the kind of man who kicks puppies and plucks the wings off butterflies."

"Is that your idea of evil behavior? You *are* an innocent!"

"Am I? Then I dare say I should like to remain so." She tied off the ends of the bandage and stood up. "That should hold, I think, until you may at least reach your home and have it properly attended."

Gavin flexed his elbow a bit to test her work and had to admit his arm felt much better than it had before. He was beginning to feel a bit more like himself, and his temper was much improved.

"Where did you learn to tie a bandage in such a manner?" he asked.

"My husband," she replied, as she gathered up the tattered remnants of the bedsheet. "He, too, often found himself in a fight over a bet or a sporting event. I often bandaged the outcome."

His dark brows came together. "That sounds hardly the job for a woman like you."

Julia shrugged her slim shoulders. "There was no one else to do it sometimes." Her expressive eyes traveled over the scars etched on his chest and shoulders. "Who bandages *your* wounds?"

"My valet serves all my needs very ably."

"You are not thinking of having him tend this wound, too, are you?"

"Of course!"

"But you really should have a surgeon to stitch it up." She placed her small hand on his good arm to draw his attention, and said impulsively, "Promise me you shall have a surgeon examine you."

A barking retort hovered on the tip of his tongue, but one look into Julia's green eyes so filled with honest and earnest concern and the words died away. She was looking down at him in such an appealing manner that he felt his gaze linger appreciatively over her face. He recalled himself and said rather grudgingly, "I shall make no promises!"

Julia didn't argue the point. Instead, she took the basin of water to the door and stepped outside to dump it. When she came back in, the duke's eyes were upon her, examining her every detail and intently watching her as she busily tidied the cottage.

Absently, he reached over to grasp the bottle, and he gave its contents a slight swirl. Ignoring the teacup, he put the bottle to his lips and poured a good quantity of bourbon into his mouth. After a few more swallows, and with his arm feeling better, he was much more like his usual self ... and he found that his gaze settled much more favorably on the little redhead with the porcelain skin.

No sooner did that spark of attraction spring to life, than he ruthlessly doused it. From habit, his taste in women ran toward serving maids and married women, females who were well up to snuff and knew the rules of the game. At all costs, he steered away from women like Julia Pettingale.

"I should have left when I found you were here," he muttered.

His words were low and grudging, but Julia heard them. "Left? Why? Surely there is nothing wrong with two strangers seeking shelter from a storm?"

"Did it never occur to you that the stories whispered about me are true? Did you never doubt whether I can be trusted to be alone with you?"

He was looking at her in an odd way that sent her heart fluttering, but she managed to say with admirable calm,

"I am not at all afraid of you, if that is what you mean. If people whisper about you the sort of things I think they whisper, I have nothing to fear. A man such as you would never find interest in a female such as me."

His dark gaze swept over her, covering every inch of her, from the top of her auburn curls to the tips of her riding boots. "Are you certain of that?" he asked, and he watched as a flush of color crept over her smooth, fair cheeks.

It had been a long time since he had seen a lady blush; the women with whom he usually associated had long since relied upon a rouge-pot to bring a bloom of color to their cheeks. But there was nothing artificial, he judged, about Julia Pettingale. She looked at him, her clear, green eyes gone slightly wide with surprise, her cheeks glowing rosily. For a moment—for just a moment—he was charmed.

"Never mind," he said, and he downed the last of the contents from the bottle. "As it happens, you are correct. I do prefer a style of woman much different from you."

"Then I am safe to wait out the storm with you."

"Do as you like, but I am leaving," he said, getting to his feet and reaching for his riding jacket. He slowly shrugged his arms into the sleeves and pulled the well-tailored lapels over his bare shoulders.

He wasn't certain the rain had stopped, but he was certain that he had to get out of that cottage. A woman like Julia Pettingale was dangerous; she was the kind of woman who made a man think of marriage and children, of playing host and hostess to the right sort of people. He hadn't entertained such thoughts in years, and he wasn't about to start entertaining them now.

He swung his caped riding coat over his shoulders and threw open the splintered door. The rain had indeed stopped. He stepped out into the early evening air, took a deep, cleansing breath of it. Behind the cottage his horse was still tethered in the shed. He led it around to the front, only to discover that Julia Pettingale was standing in the open doorway, watching him.

"You're—you're not just going to leave me here, are you?" she asked.

He steeled himself against the rather puzzled note in her voice. Instead of looking at her, he made a great show of checking his horse's bridle and reins. "I'm not going to abandon you, if that's what you mean. Stay here, and when I reach Merrifield I shall send a carriage back for you. Of course, if you prefer not to wait, you may walk back to the vicarage."

She looked out at the rain-soaked ground and at the muddy little lane that led from the cottage toward the mired road. "But it will be dark soon, and it's miles to the vicarage. You said so yourself!"

"There's only one horse, Julia," he retorted, his attention still trained on the bridle.

She was a little startled to have heard her name upon his lips, but she was even more alarmed by the prospect of being left alone in the cottage. "But it will be dark soon!" she said again.

Gavin thought he detected a note of true worry in her tone. He looked at her then, and just for a moment, he couldn't take his eyes off her. With her deep auburn hair framing her perfect complexion, and the green of her eyes providing a mirror to her thoughts, he thought she was one of the prettiest woman he had seen, and he wondered how he hadn't noticed that before.

He turned his attention back to fiddling with the bridle, then said gruffly, "You've got candles, and the fire still burns in the hearth. You've nothing to worry about."

His words had sounded harsher than he had intended, but he wasn't going to take them back. For a moment he wrestled with himself over what to do next. Common sense told him he should leave her there, that he should send a carriage back to take her to the vicarage, that he should go about his business and forget he ever met her.

But some nagging feeling within him, long dormant and unidentified, made him reluctant to do as reason dictated.

Then he made the mistake of looking at her again, and he saw that she was watching him intently, her green eyes wide and a bit apprehensive, her full lips parted as if she wanted to say more but couldn't think of any argument that might change his mind.

She looked a little helpless and very young. A feeling he judged to be compassion melted his resolve. Muffling a curse, he stomped up to the cottage. In a single, strong movement, he scooped her up in his arms and tossed her onto his horse's back.

The effort cost him. He knew immediately that his arm had started to bleed again. It certainly hurt like the devil, but it didn't pain him any more than his conscience would have, had he left her standing there.

"I'll take you home," he said gruffly, and he swung his great size up onto the horse behind her.

He didn't wait for her to answer, but set his horse to trotting, his injured arm circled about her waist, steadying her against the hard wall of his body.

Julia gasped and couldn't quite catch her breath. It took a moment for her to recover from the surprise of suddenly finding herself on horseback. "I-I cannot ride with you like this! It . . . it is most improper!"

"And you, Lady Julia Pettingale, are a most proper young woman."

"Of course!"

His arm tightened about her, and he said ruthlessly, "You may ride with me thus or you may go back to remain alone at the cottage. The choice is yours."

"I thought you intended to leave me!"

"I'm well within my rights to change my mind."

"Do you know where you're going?"

"Madam, let me remind you that *I* am not the one who was lost!"

The abrupt change in his behavior sent her head spinning. Julia turned slightly, the better to catch a glimpse of his countenance. Perhaps she could make more sense of his expression than she could of his words. She found, however, that it was inscrutable. His remarkably chiseled lips were pressed into a grim line of purpose, and his gaze was intent upon the road ahead.

"Well?" he demanded suddenly. "What have you decided?"

She started, and realized she had been staring at him. "Decided?"

"Yes. Do you like what you see, or don't you?"

Her back went straight. "You must be mistaken!"

"Of course. After all, proper young ladies do not stare at gentlemen."

She felt his arm tighten about her, pulling her ever closer against him. "*You* are no gentleman!"

"Just so."

"You are nothing but a bounder and a rogue!" she said, easily recalling all the whispered stories and rumors that had been catalogued against him.

"I am a great many things, perhaps, but never in my life have I ravished a prim-and-proper widow, so you may rest easy."

Rest easy? With the strong arms of a handsome man about her, Julia Pettingale was far from easy. Her heart was galloping wildly, and it was all she could do to keep her breath from coming in short, betraying bursts.

She felt most completely at his mercy and she wasn't quite sure whether she was exhilarated or alarmed by the notion. Yet she also knew that as long as he regarded her as a woman of prim-and-proper goodness, she had nothing to fear from him. That realization should have afforded her a measure of peace; instead, Julia was aware of a sharp prick to her vanity.

"Very well, my lord duke!" she said, her back as straight as a plank. "I see I have no other choice but to trust your judgment. I shall rely on you to see me safely back to the vicarage."

* * *

The summer sun was almost setting in the evening sky when they topped a rise and started down the other side, thereby affording Julia a full view of the impressive facade of a sprawling country mansion. She had never before come across it while riding, and she knew instinctively they were nowhere near the vicarage.

"What place is this?"

"Merrifield."

"And who is the owner of such a grand estate?"

"I am," said Gavin in a deep, even tone. "When I said I was taking you home, I meant *my* home."

Julia skewed about to look up at him in surprise. "You cannot mean to do such a thing! A bachelor residence? I cannot . . . ! Oh, I wish you had taken me to the vicarage!"

His jaw tightened. "I won't ravish you in front of the servants, if that's what's worrying you," he said darkly.

"That's not what I meant! I only meant that it isn't seemly or proper for me to . . . A bachelor residence is no place for an unattached woman!" She looked uncertainly up at him and realized too late how close his face was to hers.

He was staring at her with a darkling look that almost convinced her he could read her thoughts.

He tightened his hold about her and urged his horse forward. "If you're worried about the proprieties, I can assure you, you shall be quite safe. During the time you are a guest in my home, I shall be the very pink of gentlemanliness."

She gave his promise some thought. "Very well. I shall allow you to take me to your home, but only if you agree to send for a surgeon immediately upon our arrival so your arm may be properly examined."

For the first time since their acquaintance she heard him laugh softly.

"My dear young woman, you are not exactly in a position

to demand anything of me." Tightening his arm meaningfully about her, he added softly, "But I just may demand a few things of you."

The seductive note in his voice should have alarmed her, should have set up her defenses; instead, Julia felt a little breathless. "You . . . you promised to be a gentleman!" she reminded him.

"And so I shall be."

But he didn't ease his hold of her until they reached the front steps of the great house. Gavin drew his horse to a halt before the front entrance of Merrifield and leapt gracefully down to the ground.

A stable groom appeared from nowhere to catch the reins and hold the horse steady and two more grooms stood at hand, awaiting their master's pleasure and staring unabashedly up at Julia.

She looked down at the duke's hand, held expectantly up toward her, and a niggling of conscience caused her to hesitate. "This . . . this is really most improper and—and I should not stay alone here with you!"

"You may suit yourself, of course. But you shall have an even farther walk to the vicarage now than before." She hesitated still, and he frowned up at her. "Do you truly believe all the stories your friend whispers about me, Julia? Are you convinced I have no honor?"

"Oh, no! There is honor in everyone, even . . . !" She stopped short, aware that she had almost blundered in her reply. To make amends, she reached down to place her hand in his.

In the next moment her feet were on the ground and she was beside him, his hand at her elbow to guide her up the steps.

From the front door, the duke's butler watched them ascend the steps, an expression of patent astonishment writ upon his face. His gaze traveled from Julia to the duke and back to Julia again, and he so far forgot himself as to ask in a horrified tone what in heaven's name had occurred.

"I beg Your Grace's pardon," he said quickly, having recollected himself somewhat, "but you look as though you've been set upon! Were they footpads? A band of brigands?"

"A thunderstorm," said Gavin over his shoulder as he ushered Julia into the great hall. "Hennings, this is Lady Pettingale, who will be with us for a time this evening. Have Mrs. Crabtree attend her and— Hennings, are you listening?"

The butler, who had been staring at Julia with an expression of curiosity mixed with stunned surprise, heard the sharp tone in his master's voice. "Yes! Yes, of course!" he said, pulling himself together. "I beg Your Grace's pardon!"

"Summon Mrs. Crabtree, and have my valet attend me here in the hall."

Julia stepped forward. "And be so good as to send for a surgeon," she said, then found the duke's eyes upon her. "You promised," she reminded him.

"So I did," he said softly. "Do as Lady Pettingale asks, Hennings. Ah, Mrs. Crabtree! Take Lady Pettingale upstairs and see to her comfort, will you?"

But instead of following the housekeeper, Julia moved toward the duke, her attention fixed upon a fresh stain on the sleeve of his coat. "And you?" she asked, quite concerned. "Will . . . will you be all right?"

"I shall be upstairs myself in a moment, as soon as I have my valet attend me here. I want these boots off before I trek mud throughout the entire house." He cast her a frowning look, and said in a compelling tone, "Go with Mrs. Crabtree, Julia. I shall see you presently."

Julia obediently followed the housekeeper upstairs to a very elegantly furnished apartment. No sooner did she step across the threshold of that large, spacious room than she caught sight of her reflection in the pier glass hanging on the far wall. What she saw there stopped her in her tracks, and she stood for a moment, staring back in astonishment at her reflected image.

Even to her own kind eye she looked quite done up. Her hair had come loose from its pins in places, and tendrils of her red curls hung tangled and willy-nilly down her back. A smudge of candle soot adorned her chin. Mud was caked across the tops of her riding boots.

But her green velvet riding habit had suffered the worst damage. Pock marks speckled the shoulders and back of her velvet jacket where she had run out in the rain to fetch the bowl of water; and the duke had left some very visible mud prints along the lush fabric where he had scuffled his boots on her skirt.

"Oh, dear," she said sorrowfully. "My beautiful riding habit! It's ruined. Absolutely ruined."

Mrs. Crabtree stepped up behind her. "Begging your lady's pardon, but it's not so very bad. A good brushing will take that mud off the hems, and a gentle toweling might lessen those marks on the jacket, I think."

Julia looked doubtfully at the pitiful image that stared back at her from the mirror. "No wonder everyone was looking at me so," she murmured. "No wonder all the servants were staring! I look a horrid fright!"

"Oh, my lady, anyone can see you are a beautiful woman," said the housekeeper kindly. "You've just been through a hedgerow backwards, as the saying does go. But you're still quite lovely, if I may be so bold."

Julia shook her head slightly. "You're very kind, but I know a look of shock when I see one. And every servant who has seen me thus far has worn that very expression!"

Mrs. Crabtree's generous brows knit into a single, furrowed line. "I was hoping you would not have noticed the stares, my lady. You must forgive us, but we were so surprised when you did arrive. You see, you are the first woman our master has brought to Merrifield since our pretty little duchess died."

Julia turned quickly to look at her. "Pretty little duchess? Are you speaking of Lord Warminster's mother?"

"Oh, no, my lady! I speak of His Grace's wife. Such a beauty she was and dearer than breath. My master was only married to his pretty little duchess a little more than a year before she was taken from this world."

Julia felt her chest constrict a little. "I-I had no idea!" she uttered, a good deal surprised.

"No? Then you have not heard the rumors about my master! Or, if you have, you know them to be untrue!" She smiled upon Julia in an approving manner. "That would explain my master's behavior in bringing you here. You do seem the sort of fine lady who would never listen to horrid gossip!"

"You are very loyal to the duke." Julia was suddenly finding it difficult to think clearly.

"And why should I not be? There isn't a tenant or servant or pensioner on this estate who doesn't think the world of my master, him being so kind to us all, despite his loss."

"I had no idea," murmured Julia, finding it difficult indeed to equate the gentleman of Mrs. Crabtree's description with the surly and rude wastrel she had met at the cottage.

"No, and how could you, for I don't believe he speaks of his duchess any longer. My master is a man who won't have his wounds touched, you see."

"But I never dreamed . . . There are all those stories about him, you see—"

"Bah! Stories!" said Mrs. Crabtree contemptuously. "I know how the villagers speak ill of His Grace, and let them, I say. We at Merrifield know the truth! His grace may not be the perfect gentleman when he is out in the world, but when he comes home to Merrifield, my master is as kind and good and thoughtful a man as ever walked the earth. Surely, my lady, you are acquainted a little with that side of him!"

Was she? Every whispered story Julia had chanced to

overhear about the duke pointed to a man of wickedness. Even her friend Harriet had repeated in hushed tones stories that cast the Duke of Warminster in the light of a man decidedly evil.

But now that she came to think of it, Julia realized that a truly wicked man would have pressed his advantage during the time they were alone together in that little cottage. A ruthless man would have ridden away after the rain had stopped, leaving her alone to fend for herself.

But most importantly, an evil man would never have lifted her up before him on his horse or wrapped his wounded arm so securely yet gently about her.

"I-I suppose I am acquainted a little with that side of his character," said Julia, and she was immediately rewarded with a smile from Mrs. Crabtree. "I wonder how the duke ever came to be so misjudged?"

"How do any such stories ever come to be?" countered the housekeeper. "Now, my lady, if you will allow me to help you out of that jacket and skirt, I might be in a way of setting some of the damage back to rights. Leave everything to me!"

As Mrs. Crabtree set to work on repairing Julia's riding habit, the duke's valet, John Newley, was attempting to restore order to his master's dress. He had assisted the duke with his bath and had examined and then rebandaged his wounded arm, pronouncing that it probably did, indeed, require sewing, but if His Grace would allow him, he could no doubt stitch the thing up himself.

"You've stitched more of my wounds and set too many of my broken bones for me to trust anyone's skill but yours," said Gavin, "but not this time, I think. Hennings has sent for a physician to do the business."

Newley stiffened. "A physician? Begging your pardon, Your Grace, but who gave Hennings leave to do so?"

"I did. We thought the wound required expert treatment."

"Begging your pardon again, but *we* decided nothing of the sort," said Newley with dignity.

"No, of course not. It was Lady Pettingale who made the suggestion that I have a doctor in."

"May I be so bold as to ask why? If Your Grace doesn't think I have the touch for this sort of business, may I remind Your Grace that it was a physician who set that broken collarbone of yours at half staff; and a cripple he would have made of your arm, too—not to mention a hunchback!—had I not come along after and reset the whole business!"

"Yes, yes! I recall that very well!"

"May I also remind Your Grace that no one has tended after your scrapes and scratches but me from the time you were well nigh a boy?"

"I know that, too. I need no such reminder, in fact, but the thing of it is, I made a promise."

"It will take me only a moment to gather up everything I need," said his valet stubbornly.

Lord Warminster hesitated. "No, we'll do it later this evening when the physician arrives. For now, help me finish dressing so I may be on my way."

"On your way?" echoed Newley, once again roused to great feeling. "Your Grace is in no condition to go anywhere!"

"Nonsense!"

"You've lost blood," Newley said with a frown, "and you'll be weak as a kitten in not too much time if you don't rest."

"Stubble it! I intend to go no further than my own drawing room. Now, drat you, help me finish dressing!"

But instead of the finely tailored evening coat the duke intended to wear, his valet held up a length of black silk that had been fashioned into a sling.

Gavin's dark brows came together. "What the devil is that for?"

"It is for you to wear so your arm will be held still. To prevent further injury, Your Grace."

"Have you gone daft? She'll think I'm an infant to be mollycoddled."

"Who shall think such a thing, Your Grace?"

Gavin pointedly ignored that question, saying forcefully, "I won't wear it! It's a sign of weakness."

"I should have thought it was a sign of common sense," said Newley impudently.

"Damn you, man! Do you want her to think I've been brought to my knees by a simple sword wound? Take that thing away and help me with my coat."

When at last the duke entered the drawing room to join Julia, the offending sling had been disposed of and he was attired to his liking in a finely tailored evening coat and vest.

But Julia was not awaiting him in the drawing room, and he entered to find it empty. For a moment—but only a moment—he assured himself—he felt a pang of disappointment.

A great fire had been set to glowing in the hearth, and candles had been lit about the room to lend it a soft, warm glow. On a side table sat a tray of wines, and he had just finished pouring out a glass of claret when the door opened and Julia entered the room.

She was still in her green riding habit, which, under Mrs. Crabtree's ministrations, showed considerably less damage than it had a mere half-hour before. On her feet were a pair of borrowed slippers, and her hair, having long since lost the majority of the pins needed to hold its heavy length in place, had been simply brushed out and tied with a ribbon to trail down her back.

The effect, he thought, was charming. She looked young and lovely and very beautiful. Again he wondered how on earth he had ever thought differently before.

It was several moments before he could force himself to speak. He said rather stiffly, "I've sent a messenger to the vicarage to let them know you are here. Of course, if you don't care to wait for your friends to come and collect you, my carriage is at your disposal."

Julia took a few more steps into the room. "I am perfectly content to wait for Harriet and her husband."

He turned his back to her then, and busied his hands with the wine decanters. When he had poured out a glass for her, he crossed the brief distance between them with a few easy strides.

"A mild ratafia," he said, as she took a sip. "Sit down, won't you, and be comfortable."

Julia shunned the stylish armchairs and sank instead onto an overstuffed hassock drawn close in front of the fireplace. "I probably shouldn't drink this without having something to eat first," she said ingenuously. "I am not at all used to drinking wines."

Gavin drew a chair forward and sat down with his own glass cradled in his hands. "If you mean to enter society, you shall have to develop a taste for the stuff. Surely you drink wine with dinner at home."

"At the vicarage we are served nothing stronger than a cider. Harriet's husband fears he would set a poor example if he were to imbibe."

"I am not at all surprised," he said scornfully.

"Please don't speak cruelly of the vicar. He has been very kind to me, you know."

"I can imagine he has been—in between sermons on the proper manner in which you must disport yourself."

"I won't allow you to think ill of the Reverend Mr. Clouster. I owe him a tremendous debt. He allowed Harriet to invite me into their home when no one else would."

"And in exchange, you undoubtedly must listen to him sermonize—" He stopped short, his attention arrested. "When no one else would?"

Julia's chin managed to go up a notch, and she said in a tone of unconcern, "Very few people, I discovered, are willing to take in a penniless widow."

"Why did you not go home, then?"

"I have no home. As I told you, I have nothing of value."

"Not even a home? I don't believe it! You were born to the manor!"

"But I was not married from the manor," she countered in an even voice that held not the least trace of emotion, "and therein, you see, lies the mischief."

Gavin smiled slightly as he realized, at last, the meaning of her words. "Well, well, well! So the prim and proper Lady Julia Pettingale was married over the anvil! I would never have guessed it of you!"

She laughed softly. "Are you very much shocked?"

"I am indeed. When I think of how many times today I have listened to your maxims of propriety, I can scarce believe it!"

"It is true, I'm afraid," she said rather ruefully. "My father disapproved of the man I had chosen to marry— with good reason I discovered too late. But at the time, I was quite convinced that my father was merely acting out of cruelty. I thought at the time he opposed the marriage because his pride was at stake, because I was the only person who had ever dared defy Sir Walter Gardner."

Gavin looked at her in surprise. "Your father is Sir Walter Gardner?" She nodded, and he said, "I'm a little acquainted with him. If I'm not mistaken, he owns the finest stable in England."

"Have you bought one of his horses?"

"No, but he's offered on several occasions to buy one of mine. He wants my grey, but I have no intention of selling it to him. I must say, though, that he has been tenacious in his offers."

She smiled slightly. "My father can be very persistent."

"And was he persistent in trying to dissuade you from marrying?"

"Yes, but I wouldn't listen to him. The day I left his house with William was the day my father pledged to have nothing more to do with me."

Julia would have thought the passage of time would have enabled her to speak of that long-ago day with perfect equanimity, but no sooner had those words left her lips than she was quite forcibly reminded of the last time she had seen her father. She missed him, and longed to see him, and she felt the disarming prick of tears at the backs of her eyes.

She fought against her betraying emotions by forcing a smile and saying, "I had some jewels and some money of my own that I had inherited from my mother when she died. I thought that was all I needed in life, so I eloped with William. As it happened, William cared more for my money and jewels than he did for me."

Gavin favored her with a hard, probing stare. "Are you telling me your husband squandered your inheritance?"

"Every last groat, I'm afraid."

"Your husband was a bounder," he said bluntly.

"He didn't mean to be. Over the four years of our marriage, William eventually took everything I had, but he always thought he could win the money back if only he had a lucky turn of the cards or a bet on the right horse. But in the end, only the men with whom he gambled at Watier's profited."

"Your husband was a member at Watier's?"

"Yes, he was. Did you meet him there? I would not be at all surprised if you did for the place was practically a second home for him. He was quite good friends with some of the members: Lord Elphinham and Mr. Dobney were two fast friends of his."

Gavin conjured up a vague recollection of an eager young Tulip who had crossed his path at the club years before. "He didn't belong there, if he's the chap I think he is."

"I would have thought he could have been a crony of yours," said Julia in some surprise. "He aspired toward the Corinthian set and was quite horse-mad."

"Your husband was no more a crony of mine than the

man in the moon. Men like Elphinham and Dobney are nothing more than Peep 'o Day boys who think it smart to get swine-drunk and cause mischief. Your husband may have aspired to the Corinthian set, but if he fell in with men such as Elphinham and Dobney, it's more like he found amusement in boxing the Watch and kicking up larks and gambling his way into Dun territory."

Julia looked at him blankly. "And you don't do such things?"

"You *do* have a poor opinion of me, don't you?" he asked, in a voice that was more amused than angry. "No, I do not do such things."

Julia looked away for a moment. At last she said very thoughtfully, "William was so intent upon aping any man he thought of fashion, he never stopped to consider the consequences."

"You married a mere boy, Julia," said Gavin, his gaze intent upon her.

She wasn't quite sure what surprised her more: the use of her Christian name or the gentleness of his tone. She decided not to scold him for speaking to her so and smiled slightly. "But I, you see, was a mere girl."

His gaze traced the silhouette of her riding habit. "You're not a mere girl any longer."

The tone of his voice left Julia feeling suddenly a little breathless and a good deal disarmed. She didn't know if it was his willing and sympathetic ear or his unexpected compliment that was her undoing, but once again did she find herself close to tears. She closed her eyes, trying to block out any emotion, but it was too late. The tears were on her lashes before she could halt them.

Gavin saw them and reacted without thinking. He dropped to one knee on the floor in front of her and wrapped his good arm about her to draw her to the muscled expanse of his chest. He thought she'd resist, but she didn't. She merely allowed him to press her against him as she gave herself up to her tears.

It had been a long time since he had held a woman so tenderly. She was soft and pliant, and she smelled of sweetness and violet water. She moved slightly and bumped his sore arm, but he didn't care; he would have let her bump it a hundred times if it meant he could go on holding her.

But after only a moment in his arms, Julia pulled away and dashed at her moist eyes with the tips of her slim fingers. "I am sorry! I cannot think what came over me! I haven't cried like that since I last saw my papa!"

"Then perhaps it was time you did."

She looked quickly up at his face still so close to hers, thinking she had detected a note of sarcasm in his voice. "William took everything! Everything! Even my jewels were sold to pay his horrid debts! And after all that—after he took every last item that was dear to me!—William died and now I am alone and— Oh!" Her chin quivered threateningly, and she fought to control it.

"Go home to your father, Julia," said Gavin softly.

"I cannot! He—he disowned me! When I left his house, we said some hateful things. He will never take me in! I don't suspect you can ever understand!"

"I expect I understand perfectly well," he said, regarding her with an odd expression on his face. "Merely because time has passed does not mean you cannot still feel the pain of losing someone. Would you admit that is a fair assessment?"

"You *do* understand!" she said faintly, and she dipped her head to hide the tears that again filled her eyes.

"I'm not an idiot. Did you love him?"

The abruptness of his question brought her head up with a snap. "I-I beg your pardon?"

"My question was plainly spoke. Did you love your husband?"

"No," she said sadly, "yet that fact made it no less difficult when he died. Without William, I have no one."

"I know what it is like to be left behind. Here—let me get you off the floor."

He clasped her hand and drew her to her feet beside him. Julia looked to see his darkly guarded expression. She felt a kinship with him, an unexpected bond, and she said tentatively, "I am sorry you lost your wife."

No sooner had those tender words left her lips than his features hardened. "Don't be," he retorted. He crossed the room to the wine tray and poured out a fresh glass.

Undeterred, Julia said softly, "Sometimes grief can change a person's character."

He stared unseeing at the decanter of wine for a moment, then swung about to face her. "Is that what you think? That I was a good and honest man before I married—and then buried!—my wife? You *are* an innocent, Lady Julia Pettingale! I have been a libertine and a sharp since I first cut my teeth. Haven't you heard? According to rumor, my behavior is so depraved, even Prinny is fearful of consorting with me!"

"I am not afraid of you," she said simply.

"Maybe you should be. My history with women is from sterling."

"I know nothing of that part of your history. But if you are judging yourself harshly because your wife died . . ."

"It's my fault she is dead," he said, and his eyes, hard as agates, watched for her reaction. "I am to blame for it as surely as if I put my fingers about her throat."

"I cannot bring myself to believe that of you," she said softly.

"I can hardly believe it of myself sometimes. But I am not now the man I was years ago. In my grass days I was the same sort of bounder your husband had been. And when I married—again like your husband—I didn't change my ways. I was still a Neck-or-Nothing and mad for sport. And then one day I set my wife up on the seat beside me in my first perch phaeton. The roads were icy—I should have known—" He stopped short and set his mouth into a tight, grim line. After a moment, he squared his shoulders and said, quite angry, "Everything you have heard about me is true. There! You may now repeat with authority all the stories you have been told about me!"

"I don't repeat gossip," Julia said very quietly. "I dare say the village is rife with stories that feature you in some sort of scandalous behavior, but I would never believe such stories if they were spoken to me. I am a very good judge of character, and I would judge you are not as unsavory a man as you would wish me to believe."

"Is that so? We shall see if you may be made to alter that opinion."

He crossed the space between them with purposeful strides that sent Julia's nerves fluttering. Suddenly, she was unsure whether she was safe alone with him or in significant peril. She had only an instinct that he was, at heart, an honorable man, but her instincts also told her that he fought very hard to be otherwise.

He proved that theory by reaching out to lightly cup one hand against the softness of her cheek. The touch of his palm against her skin startled her. She looked up at him, her green eyes wide, and her body reacting as if it were suddenly on fire.

She thought he meant to kiss her; indeed, he lowered his head slightly, but his lips stopped just short of hers.

"Shall we see if you can be made to alter your ever-optimistic opinion of me?" he asked, sending the warmth of his breath dancing against her face.

Julia swallowed hard and said in a voice barely above a whisper, "I-I have heard nothing yet that will change my mind!"

"Are you certain?" he asked very quietly, and he watched her green eyes widen slightly. "Are you that convinced you know me so well, Julia Pettingale?"

"Yes," she answered at once.

That was not the answer he had anticipated, and he dropped his hand and stepped back from her in surprise.

But the frown returned to his brow quickly. He gave his head a slight shake. "Lord, you can drive a man to madness."

Julia had no idea what he meant by such an accusation, but she was given no opportunity to question him over it. He moved away from her, and as he did so, the door of the sitting room burst opened.

Without announcement or preamble the Reverend Mr. Clouster and his wife, Harriet, sailed into the room, still possessed of their cloaks, hats and gloves.

"Julia, we have come to take you home!" said the vicar, in a loud and forceful tone, as if he expected to meet with opposition. "We came as soon as we received news you were here!"

Harriet swept up to Julia and gave her a quick hug, then held her by the shoulders, saying earnestly, "My dear friend, you look a fright! Your eyes were like saucers just now when we came in and your face— My dear, you look as though you had been made to suffer the most beastly shock!" She cast a sidelong glance at the duke and said, in a meaningful voice, "I hope, my dear, you have been quite *safe*."

"Harriet, leave this to me," said the young vicar, fully mindful of his duty. He squared his shoulders and faced the duke with purpose. "Warminster, I-I demand to be told what occurred here today. I demand to know what outrage you meant to commit by abducting this young woman."

"There has been no outrage, Clouster, and no abduction, so save your breath," said Gavin dampeningly.

"So say you! But I dare say Julia may have a different notion. If any harm has come to her, I-I shall knock you down, Warminster!"

Gavin drew his imposingly muscled body up to its full height. "You may certainly try."

Julia shook off Harriet's hold and stepped between the

two men. "No! There shall be no fighting! You must believe me when I say nothing untoward occurred today."

"Julia," said the vicar sternly, "I know of what sort of behavior this man is capable. I also know your innocence is no match for his wiles."

"You are mistaken," Julia insisted. "The duke has been very kind to me."

The Reverend Mr. Clouster looked suspicious. "Is that true, Warminster? Nothing occurred out of place?"

"Are you doubting the lady's word, Clouster?"

The vicar was not a man who relished the notion of a physical confrontation—especially a confrontation with a man of the duke's size and reputation—but he was determined to do the right thing by Julia. He drew himself up and said, doggedly, "Warminster, do I have your assurance or don't I?"

"For what it's worth," said Gavin, "yes. You have my assurance that nothing untoward occurred."

"And you have my assurance, as well," said Julia.

Harriet came forward then to clasp her hands in an earnest grip. "Thank heavens! When I think of what might have happened . . . ! Only we shall not speak of that now for you are too modest, too innocent, to believe anything but good may exist in the world!" She wrapped an arm about Julia's shoulders and began to lead her toward the door. "Our carriage is outside, my dear. We shall have you home straightaway. Then you may forget all about this unpleasant and unfortunate business!"

"But, Harriet, it wasn't unpleasant, and it certainly wasn't unfortunate. In fact, I should venture to say it was great of piece of luck that the duke should have come upon me in the thunderstorm!" Julia shook off Harriet's hold and turned toward Gavin, unwilling to leave without proving to Harriet and her husband that they were wrong about him.

But he had turned away to stand at the side table where he poured out another glass of wine. When he was done and turned back toward her, he favored Julia with no more than the merest and coolest of nods.

It was difficult indeed for Julia to believe that the duke could look upon her with such coldness when only moments before he had held her and comforted her with exquisite tenderness. But she had no opportunity to dwell on the change in him, for Harriet had renewed her efforts to guide Julia toward the door. She draped an arm about Julia's shoulders and led her relentlessly out into the hallway and down the stairs.

Only when they were in the Clousters' carriage and at last on their way to the vicarage did anyone speak again. Then it was Harriet who ventured to say, "My dearest friend, you may tell me the truth. Was the duke—was he quite odious? Did he subject you to his unwanted attentions? You may feel free to confide it to me!"

"Harriet, I assure you, nothing of the kind occurred!"

"But when we came upon you just now, you were standing so close together, I thought perhaps . . . Well, I thought perhaps he might have taken advantage of your situation. He is, after all, a man capable of the most horrid behavior!"

Julia refused to believe it. "Harriet, you are a dear friend, but I wish you would not repeat such vile gossip!"

"It isn't merely gossip," said the vicar gravely. "My dear, Julia, you are a friend and so I must tell you: the Duke of Warminster is not a man to be trusted. His past actions and his present behavior are not those of an honorable gentleman. He is a known libertine!"

Harriet placed one gloved hand over Julia's arm and gave it an affectionate squeeze. "Of course, you're so good and dear that you cannot imagine anyone having as questionable a reputation as the duke enjoys. I blame myself. I should have warned you of him when you first arrived. I should have told you to avoid his presence at all costs. I should have—"

"You should have told me he had been married," said

Julia, and she watched Harriet and the vicar exchange startled glances.

"We don't usually speak of that," said Mr. Clouster, "for the story of Warminster's marriage is one of far-reaching tragedy and sadness."

"Dear Julia, before you feel the least bit of sympathy for the man, you must be made aware of the facts," said Harriet. "Yes, he was married, my dear; but, you see, it is rumored that his wife died by his hand."

"That rumor is not true!" protested Julia.

"We have no manner in which to confirm or deny the story, but there is a very strong suspicion in the neighborhood over the circumstances of the duchess's death," said the vicar. "Warminster has been taking up and then discarding women ever since—although not, I grant you, with the same degree of ruthlessness."

"Has . . . has he had many women?" Julia asked, and suddenly wished she hadn't.

"Quite a few, as I've been told," said the vicar. "If only half the rumors concerning his behavior are to be believed, the duke does everything to excess—gambling, drinking. I doubt very much that women are an exception to that rule."

Julia became aware of a sudden trembling in her body, as if within her a war waged between her usually sensible brain and her now-rampant emotions. Common sense told her an entire village full of people could not be wrong, that there had to be some element of truth to the many rumors concerning the Duke of Warminster's character. From his own lips did she have evidence that he moved in a circle of those she most abhorred, a circle of gamblers and drinkers and men who placed more import on sport than on the decent comfort of their families and homes— men who were just as her husband had been.

Yet some niggling feeling persisted that everything she had learned about him was untrue. She said, in a voice barely above a whisper, "There must be some mistake! He told me himself— Oh, I don't know what to believe!"

Harriet clasped her hands over Julia's in a meaningful grip. "Julia dear, you know we have only your welfare at heart. It is very admirable that you have so much goodness that you should want to defend a man of Warminster's ilk. How very like you! But you must not dwell upon what has occurred here this evening."

"Harriet is right. It is best we say no more about this unfortunate episode," pronounced the vicar. "If anyone were to discover you were in that man's company, you would never recover!"

"It's true, you know," said Harriet. "You would be quite ruined if it were known that you associated with the duke, to say nothing of having spent time alone with him!"

"But it was all so innocent!" said Julia.

"I know, my dear. Yet it would be so simple for someone to misinterpret what occurred. After all, two people, quite alone, and one of them enjoying a most scandalous reputation . . ." Harriet allowed her voice to trail off meaningfully.

The vicar fixed Julia with a stern look. "Your first—and only!—encounter with the Duke of Warminster is over, Julia. For your sake, and the sake of your reputation, we must never speak of it again. Thankfully, the odds are against any chance that his path shall ever again cross yours."

Three days later, in the drawing room at the vicarage, Julia Pettingale pinned a length of borrowed ribband to the sleeves of one of her oft-worn evening gowns, then stepped back to study the effect.

Harriet looked up from the book she was reading and said approvingly, "That will look very smart, my dear. How clever of you to think of making your old gowns look new, merely by adding a bow here or there."

Julia, too, was pleased. "I was certain the blue of the ribband would go very well with this dress. Thank you, Harriet, for lending it to me."

"It is not a loan, my dear; you may keep the ribband, with my blessing. I hope it may bring you luck."

"I shall need more than luck if I am to find a husband among the gentlemen attending the village assemblies," said Julia sensibly. "You will be sure, won't you, to point out to me the most eligible of men?"

"Of course! I dare say there are any number of local gentlemen who shall make very nice husbands. One, in particular, should suit you very well, I think. He is quite handsome and of a very happy disposition."

"He sounds very much like the sort of man I should like to meet. Does this paragon have a name?" asked Julia.

"He is Mr. Worthing, and since there have been any number of young ladies on the scramble for him over the years, you may count yourself lucky if he should take you in regard. Of course, you are quite the prettiest young woman to come into our village in some time, and your disposition is so sunny. I should think that in little time you shall find yourself surrounded by suitors, including Mr. Worthing. Your social success—at least in our little neighborhood—is assured!"

"Gracious!" said Julia, laughing. "If I am to be such a success, I think I would be wise to embellish some more of my old gowns!"

"You said that in jest, but I think it an excellent notion. Do let me help!" begged Harriet with enthusiasm. "I know the very thing! I have an old sewing basket in which I often used to save bits of lace and ribbands. And if I remember correct, I kept in it, too, a very cunning length of gold torsade; just the thing, I think, for your blue satin evening dress. Now, let me see . . . Where *did* I put that basket?"

"I have no idea, but now that I have heard of its treasures, I shall certainly help you find it," offered Julia, smiling.

"Nonsense! I believe I recall seeing it in my dressing

room not too long ago. Now, you continue on stitching the ribbands to your gown while I go find the basket. I shall be back in a wink!''

As it happened, she was gone for a considerably longer period of time, and when the door to the drawing room opened at last, Julia fully expected to see her friend march into the room and triumphantly present the sewing basket. Instead, Harriet's housemaid stepped into the room and announced, in reverential accents, the Duke of Warminster.

"The duke!" Julia repeated, jumping to her feet. "Heavens, are you quite certain?"

The maid responded by swinging wide the door. Julia had time only to tuck an errant curl beneath her morning cap before Lord Warminster swept into the room.

It had been three days since Julia had left Merrifield in the Clouster's coach, three days in which she had thought of the duke and wondered over him. Now that he stood before her, she had to fight back an unexplained swell of emotion and a sudden bout of breathlessness.

Her eyes flew to his face. She detected there no sign of the grim and harsh lines she had noticed the last time they were together. Instead, there was a hint of expectancy about his expression, as if he were on watch to her reaction at seeing him again.

She dipped a very circumspect curtsy and said in a tolerably composed voice, "Good morning!"

"Good morning," he replied. "I didn't startle you just now, I hope."

"Not at all!" she replied, maintaining her composure. "I see you are much improved from the last time I saw you. Is your arm better?"

"Decidedly. You did a fine job of patching it up."

She managed a laugh, saying, "No thanks to you! You were a wretched patient, you know. But now that your arm has healed sufficiently, I shall at last have the answer to a question that has been plaguing me for the last three days."

"What question is that?"

"Whether it is your habit to be difficult . . . or was it your wound that made you so surly and unpleasant?"

His dark brows flew skyward in momentary surprise, but he said quite temperately, "I am always unpleasant. Didn't you know?"

"Oh, yes!" she answered, unable to cudgel her brain into forming a more sensible reply. She did manage to recall her manners, however, and invited him to sit down. Too late did she realize the dress she had been repairing was spread across the chair.

"Oh, dear! Let me move that for you." Nervously, she gathered up the gown.

"Do not let me interrupt your work," he murmured politely.

"This? Why it is only an old gown I have been reworking so I may wear it again to the assembly. I've added bows to the sleeves, you see. It is nothing, really!"

He cast her an odd look. "Adding bows to a nightgown might be nothing; adding bows to a dress to make it fashionable is another matter altogether, in my opinion."

She stiffened. "When I confided in you my present circumstance, I never dreamed you would one day make sport of it."

"You mistake. Your circumstance, as you call it, rubs too much against my grain for me to make sport of it." His eyes settled upon her. "What's that on your head?"

She started, and her fingertips flew to her cap, fully expecting to find a spider or some other equally distasteful object lurking there. Patting frantically about, she found nothing out of the way, and raised questioning eyes toward his. "Why? What—what do you see?"

"I see a dreadful bit of cloth covering your hair. Why are you wearing it?"

"My cap? Why . . . why, I am a widow and—"

"You were not wearing it the other day when we met."

"No, no, I wasn't."

"It covers your hair."

She smiled slightly. "I believe it is intended to do just so!"

"You are much more to my liking without it."

She should have blushed; she should have scolded him for speaking to her so; instead, she felt again that same breathlessness she had experienced when first he had entered the room. It was a difficult thing indeed to equate the wastrel Julia had met three days earlier with the man now standing before her. It was just as impossible to believe that a man who freely admitted to engaging in duels and riding roughshod over the laws of the land was one and the same as the man who had haunted her thoughts from the moment their paths had crossed.

She tugged the cap a bit lower over her ears and said rather shakily, "I should never have ventured out without it, as if I were a young girl not yet out in the world. It was wrong of me not to have been wearing it when first we met."

He frowned. "I suppose you had that from your friend."

Her chin came up. "Yes. Harriet was good enough to remind me that a widow in my position must observe all the proprieties."

"In your position? What do you mean?"

"I mean that I intend to reenter society and I must, therefore, strive to be circumspect in all things."

"I see. Will you reenter society in London, or here in the village?"

"I am afraid London is out of the question, but Harriet has promised that she and her husband shall conduct me to all the village functions. I shall attend musicales and assemblies, and I shall dance and play cards and delight in every entertainment put before me!"

"So you intend to make up for lost time, do you?"

"Indeed, I do!"

"And catch the eye of some eligible bachelor?"

"As many bachelors as possible!" she answered, with a slight smile.

His dark brows came together. "Is that your plan, then, Julia? To marry again?"

She was suddenly unable to meet his eyes, and she made a great show of smoothing the wrinkles from the gown as it hung over her arm. "Yes. Yes, it is," she said.

"I see. And how will you choose between your suitors? Will you marry the most wealthy of them so you may at last have some of your fortune restored you?"

That brought her head up quickly. "You make me sound quite mercenary!"

"Aren't you?"

"Certainly not!" she said, her temper rising. "How can you speak to me so? You know I have nothing in this world—nothing at all!"

"And can you think of no other way to remedy your situation than to marry?"

"No," she said a little sadly. "I have no means of supporting myself, I am afraid, and I have lived too long off the kindness of friends."

"You could make peace with your father," he suggested. "You could go to him."

"He won't have me. Don't you think I tried?"

"So it must be marriage, then. I hope you may get what you want out the business."

She felt herself stiffen again. "I shall not make demands, you know, and I am not overly nice in my requirements. All I ask for is a man of sense for a husband, one who will provide me with a place to live. In return, I shall provide him with a home that is refined and peaceful—"

"And boring," interpolated Gavin.

"If the security of having a roof over my head is boring," she answered tersely, "then I am content to be bored."

"You will marry for the wrong reasons, Julia."

"Will I? You, I suppose, are an expert in such things!"

"Expert enough to know that I shall never marry again—for any reason!"

"I do not share that luxury," she retorted. There had been something, she thought, a little hurtful in the way he had spoken to her. She turned her back to him then and made a great show of folding up the gown she had been sewing, then gathered up her needles and threads and ribbands.

Gavin silently watched her move about the room. Until he had made her acquaintance, it had been a long time since he had found himself in the company of a woman of Julia Pettingale's caliber. Too long. He had forgotten how pleasing it was to see a woman move with gentle beauty. He had a sudden vision of her, gowned in finest silk and moving with easy grace from one guest to another in a crowded drawing room. His drawing room.

His gaze dwelled appreciatively on her. As she had been the first time he had met her, she was dressed very simply in a gown that was rather out of date; yet she wore it with a certain air of elegance that was unmistakable. No baubles or jewels graced her ears or the slender column of her throat, nonetheless he thought she held her head in the same regal way she might have borne it had she been adorned with the crowned jewels of a queen.

His gaze traveled upward—upward to where that wretched cap covered her hair. He wanted nothing more than to pluck the thing off her head.

He couldn't think of a single reason why he shouldn't.

Gavin closed the distance between them in a few easy strides, and before Julia could turn about, before she even realized he was there behind her, he pulled the cap from her head.

Julia swung around, her eyes wide and her lips parted in surprise. Her hair had been pinned up into a profusion of curls beneath the cap; now freed, the fiery tendrils caught the light of the sun as it streamed through the window, making her hair look so soft, so appealing, that his fingers itched to touch it. In the soft light of the morning, her skin was like porcelain, perfect and clear. It would have been so easy for him to reach out and touch her. She was so close, he could see the little flecks of gold in the depths of her wide, green eyes. And she looked right back at him, saying nothing.

Before he could think, before he knew what he was doing, he was reaching for her. "I can't fight this anymore," he said, almost beneath his breath. If his voice was gruff and grudging, his lips, when they brushed hers, were tenderness itself.

Her mouth was soft and inviting beneath his, and he took his time kissing her, savoring every moment. Then slowly, alert to her reaction, he changed the tenor of their kiss, deepening it until he held her completely in his power. His hands moved slowly over her, spanning her narrow waist, pressing her against him, willing her to kiss him back.

Julia didn't disappoint him. She threw her arms up around his neck and returned his kiss wholeheartedly. She had never kissed a man back before. Having been taught that ladies were merely passive recipients of such passions, she had never even kissed her husband when he had been alive, but she wanted to kiss Gavin. She wanted to return to him a small amount of the pleasure he was giving her.

After a moment he raised his head and looked down at her. "You've never been kissed that way before, have you?" he asked.

"Never," she answered, feeling a little light-headed.

"Not even by your husband?"

"No."

He looked down at her; at the kiss-bruised lips raised so enticingly toward his. He tightened his arms about her and whispered, "William Pettingale was a fool."

Julia wasn't sure what exactly he was talking about, but she heartily wished he would stop talking altogether and just kiss her again.

She was to have her wish. Gavin's mouth met hers once more, and this time, his kiss was long and lingering and tender. Unlike anything she had ever experienced, it left her hungry for something more.

After several more minutes of such heaven, Gavin raised his head. Slowly, and more than a bit reluctantly, he loosened his hold of her and stepped away. "God, what you do to me . . ."

Julia watched him move very pointedly toward the other side of the room. Her eyes met his, and she saw that although he was regarding her rather fixedly, he was also smiling slightly. It occurred to her that he could no doubt very easily make a woman fall in love with him when he looked at her in just such a way. That thought was swiftly succeeded by the startling realization that he had just succeeded in doing exactly so.

She strongly suspected she had lost her heart to him, and she was a little bit stunned to realize that of all the men in the world, she was halfway in love with a man who had long made it his practice to scorn society and fan the flames of gossip concerning his reputation.

But the irony was, she could listen to the stories of his notorious behavior and lectures on the logic of shunning him only in his absence. When he was with her and her eyes met his, she became instantly convinced that he was an honorable man, worthy of her friendship and of her affection.

Whether or not he felt any of the same emotion for her, she had no way of discovering, for Harriet Clouster tumbled back into the drawing room then, the promised sewing basket in her arms. She was halfway across the room before she realized Warminster was there. She drew up short, and her expression dissolved into one of shock. "Duke! Gracious, I had no idea . . . ! When did you . . . ? Heavens!"

He saved her the trouble of forming a more sensible conversation by stepping forward to shake hands. "Mrs.

Clouster, how do you do?'' he asked, so politely as to stun her even further. "I have called merely to satisfy myself that Lady Pettingale was well and suffered no ill effects from our encounter earlier this week.''

"Oh, no! Julia suffered not at all and—and she is very well!'' sputtered Harriet, still quite flustered.

"I am glad to hear it,'' said Gavin. He turned and claimed Julia's hand momentarily. "Lady Pettingale, I hope I may have the pleasure of seeing you again sometime.''

Julia was reluctant to allow his fingers to slip from hers, and she heartily wished he would stay longer. "Will I not see you at any of the village parties? Mrs. Ludhill is hosting a card party this evening, and tomorrow there is to be an assembly with dancing. Will you not be there?''

"No, I never partake of neighborhood society,'' he said quietly. "I find the villagers have enough tales to tell of me without my adding any more fuel to their fires.''

He departed before Julia could think of any reason to make him stay. No sooner had the door closed upon him than Harriet directed a rather horrified gaze upon her and said, "You, Julia Pettingale, are playing with fire! You have had more than ample opportunity to hint the duke away, which is what any prudent woman would do! Instead, you invite him into my very own drawing room, as bold as you please!''

"I'm sure I don't know what you are talking about,'' said Julia, in what she thought was a voice of abject innocence. She took the sewing basket from Harriet's lifeless fingers and began sorting through its contents.

"I am talking about you and the Duke of Warminster!'' Harriet replied. "Pray, why was he here?''

"He explained the reason for his call. I believe his motives were quite gentlemanly.

"I don't!'' retorted Harriet. "I saw the way he looked at you just now, and I also noticed how you looked at him.

For heaven's sake, Julia, stop this madness before it goes any further!"

Julia, feeling her temper rise, said rather defiantly, "I have met the duke on only two occasions and in both instances, he was very kind to me. I cannot think why you have chosen to hold him in such low regard."

"Julia, the Duke of Warminster is a libertine," Harriet declared bluntly. "It pains me to say such a thing, but it is time you knew!"

"I am sure you must be mistaken!" protested Julia.

"Mistaken? Oh, no! Far from it, my dear! There are enough stories about him to fill the pages of a book! The first chapter shall describe how he has been known to gamble away a small fortune on the turn of a single card. The second chapter shall reveal that he runs sporting-mad to the exclusion of all other pursuits."

"I-I am sure you are mistaken!" Julia said again, but this time her voice was less assured. "He has never revealed such behavior to me!"

"You have only to look about the neighborhood to judge his behavior," retorted Harriet. "When he is at Merrifield, he spends his leisure time at the local inn, where his favorite drinking companion happens to be a serving maid by the name of Leggy Liz. And in London, he has a house on Albemarle Street where he has installed his latest flame! My dear Julia, this man is not for you!"

"Rumors! Gossip! I refuse to judge a man merely on stories that neither you nor I know in fact to be true!" protested Julia.

"Then here is some truth for you, Julia, and I shall speak it plainly to you, as a friend. When I invited you to visit I promised I would do my best by you to find you a husband. But you must know that no man will offer for you if it is put about that you are on intimate terms with a known libertine. For your own sake, you must end your friendship with the duke."

"No! Harriet, I cannot do that!" said Julia, truly alarmed.

"Nor do I wish to conduct myself as a prim and proper widow, circumspect in all things!"

"My dear Julia," Harriet said, a bit more kindly, "no man of honor will ever propose marriage to a woman who counts a libertine among her acquaintance." Julia was quiet for a moment, and Harriet prompted, "You do see that I am right, don't you?"

Julia knew very well that Harriet was speaking nothing but the truth, but she fought against it with a feeble protest. "I don't think you would say such things if only you knew him as I do."

"I know him well enough to realize that he will probably never offer you marriage. He can only prevent you, by association, from marrying another, and then where will you be?"

Where, indeed? In Harriet's rather direct words, Julia was forced to acknowledge a truth she would rather dismiss: she was in love with the Duke of Warminster, and had been from the moment he had set her upon his horse and wrapped his strong arm comfortingly about her. She thought since that moment she had witnessed changes in him; she had detected a softness, an unbending whenever he was in her company. But she also recalled how guarded he was of his emotions and how much he grieved still for a wife who was long gone from him.

Harriet watched the play of emotions cross Julia's face and said kindly, "My dear friend, I cannot stand by and watch you make the same mistake twice. Your first marriage was disastrous. I beg you not to doom your second marriage to the same fate."

Julia didn't have to guess at her meaning. She looked at Harriet, the light of dawning recognition in her eyes. "Heavens!" she said, sinking weakly onto a chair.

Harriet was right; the duke might never offer her marriage. He had, in fact, never once given her any indication of his feelings or allowed her to build her hopes on any loverlike words or caresses. Yet marriage was the only avenue by which Julia could obtain for herself some sort of security for the future. Without marriage, she was relegated to living off the kindness of her friends for the rest of her life.

Harriet wrapped a comforting arm about Julia's shoulders and said compellingly, "You see that I am correct, I know! Now, promise me you shall remember what I have said. If you have any hopes of marrying again, you must have nothing more to do with the Duke of Warminster! Promise me, now!"

Julia closed her eyes and fought back the small lump that had formed in her throat. She said, at last, in a voice of flat despair, "I promise. From this day forward, I shall have nothing more to do with the Duke of Warminster."

Gavin made the drive from Sussex to London in record time and reached his town house in Grosvenor Square just after the summer sun sank on the horizon. During the entire drive he had pushed his horses to their limits and had maintained a pall-mall pace that had, on more than one occasion, caused Newley to clutch his seat and hold on for dear life. But there was no time to be lost. Gavin knew that if he was going to accomplish what he had set out to do, he had to reach London before it was too late; before gentlemen of fashion left their homes for the evening; before they set off for their nightly entertainments at theatres or their clubs.

He had only a slim chance of succeeding. In truth, during the entire drive he had frequently questioned his own sanity, telling himself that Julia Pettingale meant nothing to him and that her estrangement from her father mattered to him not one jot. Still, he pushed toward London, and when at last he arrived, he left his curricle and horses standing in the street, entering the house only to order that his grey be saddled and brought round immediately.

"Your Grace is not thinking of going riding at this hour?" objected Newley as he observed the darkened sky.

"Yes, as a matter of fact, I am," retorted the duke, "and you're coming with me in the curricle. I want you to sound a certain knocker at someone's door."

Newley looked a trifle alarmed. "Drive your curricle, Your Grace? Do you think that wise? I've never driven your bays before."

"Don't worry, they lost their edge miles back. You'll only be driving to Green Street, after all, and I shall be riding alongside all the way. Never fear!"

As it happened, fear did not overtake Newley until the drive to Green Street had been accomplished and they were pulled up before a very large and elegant town house.

"Sound the knocker, Newley," commanded Lord Warminster, waiting on horseback. "Let us see if Sir Walter Gardner is at home."

Newley obediently jumped down from the curricle and did as he was told. But no sooner was his summons at the door answered, the front door having been swung wide open by the butler of that establishment, than Lord Warminster went into action. Still astride his horse, he ascended the front steps and, ducking his head, drove his mount directly into the front hall of the house.

Riding past the stunned expressions of Newley, the butler and several footmen positioned about the hall, he sent his horse cantering up the staircase. At the first floor, he reached down to open the first door he came to. That room was empty, so he rode on down the hall to the next door. Again he reached down and opened it, and this time, he found what he was looking for.

Sir Walter Gardner, unsuspecting that a man on horseback had invaded his home, was leisurely partaking of a glass of port before departing for an evening's entertainment. But when the door flew open and the Duke of Warminster rode his grey stallion into the room, he flew to his feet, oversetting his glass and sputtering with shock.

"Warminster!" he managed to say at last. "What the devil is the meaning of this!"

Gavin circled his fidgeting horse twice about the room, his dark eyes focused all the while upon Sir Walter. "Not too many days ago you told me you wanted to buy this horse. I am here to sell him to you."

"Of all the— Have you gone mad?"

"Perhaps I have, but that is not at all to the point. Do you still wish to buy him or don't you?"

"You *are* mad!" accused Sir Walter. "How dare you come to me like this!"

"I dare many things, Gardner, but I didn't come here to catalogue my exploits for you."

"No need, I assure you! Like everyone else, I am well aware that you have been barely hanging onto the hem of decent society for years."

"I'm flattered you have taken such an interest in me," said Gavin, "but I would rather we concluded this business so I may be on my way. Do you wish to purchase this animal, or don't you? The price, I assure you, is very reasonable."

Realizing at last that his uninvited guest was speaking with perfect sincerity, Sir Walter Gardner frowned as he watched the Duke of Warminster continue to circle his shying horse about the furniture. "Very well. You may name your price, but I do not doubt you have in mind some exorbitant sum!"

"On the contrary, I don't want your money, Gardner. I want your word."

Sir Walter's eyes widened. "My . . . my word?" he repeated.

"Yes. On paper," said Gavin evenly. "I will sell you this horse. You shall pay for it by writing a brief letter to your daughter."

Sir Walter stood very still for a moment, his attention arrested. Then slowly he sank down onto a chair. "You've seen her, then? You've seen my Julia? Is . . . is she well?"

"You may ask her yourself. I'm not a message boy, Gardner. Now, write the damn letter."

"No."

Gavin's horse minced warningly. "*What* did you say?"

"I shall not write a letter to my daughter—not now; not ever," Sir Walter replied stiffly. "My daughter has been dead to me for years, ever since she married that neck-or-nothing, Pettingale!"

"But she's not dead. She's in Sussex, living off the kindness of friends. She hasn't a pence to call her own."

"I-I did not know that," murmured Sir Walter with a slight shake of his head. "I had heard Pettingale had died, but she seemed afterward to merely disappear! I had no notion where she had got to."

"Nor did you ever try to discover her, I fancy. Julia deserves better from you, Gardner."

"She defied me!" countered the baronet. "She shamed me! She should never have eloped with any man, to say nothing of a man of whom I disapproved!"

"She has paid sorely for the rashness of that one decision. She has nothing, Gardner. Nothing at all! Do you intend that she should continue to pay for your wounded pride for the rest of her life? I would have taken you for a better man than that!"

Sir Walter looked up and cast a speculative glance in Gavin's direction. "And what, may I ask, is your interest in all of this? What is my daughter's situation to you?"

"Nothing. Let us merely say I have a keen dislike of seeing someone left utterly alone in the world."

"As you once were," said Sir Walter with a pointed look. He got up from his chair and slowly crossed the room to where a tray of wines and glasses had been placed on a side table. He poured out two fresh glasses of port and held one out toward Gavin. "Get off that blasted horse, Warminster."

After a moment's consideration, Gavin did just so and led the animal to where Newley and a host of other startled household servants were crammed in the door frame, watching the spectacle of a man on horseback parade about the drawing room of their lord and master. He handed the reins to Newley, saying, "Take him back down to the street. I shall meet you there, presently."

With the door shut to afford them privacy, Gavin accepted the proffered glass and found the baronet eyeing him measuringly.

"Suppose you begin," said Sir Walter, "by telling me how long you have known my daughter."

"Not long. A mere matter of days."

"I see. And you're in love with her, are you?"

Gavin frowned. "Not at all."

"I don't believe you. You are either lying or you have not yet admitted to yourself your feelings for her."

"I did not come here to discuss my feelings," said Gavin tersely.

"No, I don't suppose you did. Let me speak plainly to you, then, for I would not wish you to think I don't know what it is you're about. You think to persuade me to recognize her. You think that by doing so, she shall again stand to inherit all that I have, making her once again a wealthy woman."

"That is exactly my intent."

Sir Walter cast him a ruthless look. "I shall never recognize any marriage between you and my daughter, Warminster, nor will I ever allow my fortune to fall into your hands."

"Don't talk nonsense, Gardner. I am a wealthy man in my own right; I have no need of your fortune. As for marrying your daughter, the thought has never entered my head."

"Indeed? If you aren't in love with her, then why are you here?"

Gavin was a little startled by the question. He opened his mouth to speak, then closed it just as quickly. He had never stopped to consider why he had behaved as he did.

He suspected his impulsiveness was driven only by a deep desire to see Julia Pettingale happy. He wanted to see the look on her face when she realized her father had been restored to her; he wanted to be there when she discovered that her long and hurtful alienation from her father was over.

But now that he considered it, he realized he had yet another motive for wanting to see her united with her father: he wanted to remove from her path any incentive for marrying again. From the moment Julia had first told him of her plans to marry, he had wrestled with his feelings. Without knowing why, he had hated the thought of her marrying some respectable yet eminently dull country gentleman. Even less could he like the idea of her dancing in the arms of some respectable villager at a country assembly. It wasn't until now, under the watchful eye of the baronet, that he realized the reason for those feelings: he was afraid of losing her.

He recalled quite clearly what it was like to be in love, for he had loved his first wife very well. But he also recalled even more vividly what it was like to have lost her. He had spent any number of his most recent years behaving recklessly and avoiding at all costs any attachment that might lead to affection; he'd had no intention of ever again reliving the pain of losing a beloved wife.

But then he had met Julia Pettingale, and for the first time in years he had felt that tug of attraction that was too strong to be denied. It was beyond his power to admit that he loved her and wanted to marry her himself, but he was very well able to admit that he wished to deter her from marrying another. He said, with stunning bluntness, "It so happens, Gardner, that Julia does plan to be wed again—but not to me. She has taken it into her head that she must find and marry some country squire of, no doubt, high moral standards and infinite respectability. She sees no other way to secure her future."

"And that chafes with you, does it?" asked Sir Walter

pointedly. Having received no answer to his question, after a thoughtful moment, he said, "Well, I suppose it chafes with me, also."

"Then write to her and tell her so."

Sir Walter shook his head stubbornly. "She defied me. She was rebellious and willful."

"Having met you I see where she comes by such traits. Now, write the damn letter, Gardner!"

Sir Walter sat silently for a moment. Then, without a word, he went to a small writing table, where he set his pen to paper. When he stood again a few moments later, he folded that single sheet and, taking a candle from its holder, dripped a puddle of wax onto the fold, then set his signet ring against it.

Silently he handed the letter to Gavin. "I shall be glad to have my Julia back," he said at last. "Losing first my wife and then my daughter have been the two great sorrows of my life. When I think how much time I have wasted. . . !"

"I am glad to see you come to your senses," said Gavin.

"You shouldn't be," Sir Walter retorted, "because it's going to cost you. I trust when you rashly rode that horse of yours into this room you had already considered that you were going to have to find another way home tonight?"

"I did."

"Good, because I intend to have that grey of yours, Warminster. You offered him, and I intend to keep him. That was our bargain, wasn't it? Well, you have your letter, and now I mean to have that stallion!"

"I gave you my word," Gavin replied stiffly. "I won't go back on it now."

"Tell me, is it your practice to always keep your word?"

"If I make a promise, I keep it."

Sir Walter took his measure a moment. "One day it might come to pass that I shall discover whether you are really as odious and rash as rumor makes you out to be.

I rather think not, given your behavior here tonight. There's one more thing, Warminster, you might be in the way of doing for me, if you've a mind to.''

Gavin inclined his head. "If it is in my power, sir.''

"I wonder, Warminster,'' said the baronet, "if you would be good enough to bring my daughter home to me.''

Gavin raised his glass slightly. "It will be my pleasure, sir,'' he said. "I shall have your daughter home to you within the week. You have my word on it.''

Julia Pettingale learned, too, that the Duke of Warminster was a man of his word. He had told her he would not appear at Mrs. Ludhill's card party and he had not done so, although Julia had spent the better part of the day convincing herself that he would be there.

She had hoped to see him again; instead, she knew a keen sense of disappointment when, in the late hours of the evening, the card party was drawing to a close and still he had not made an appearance.

Nor did he appear in the vicarage drawing room the next day. Again did Julia hope to see him. She had even excused herself from paying morning calls in the neighborhood with Harriet and her husband by pleading the headache. Her excuse had fooled neither Harriet nor the vicar; certainly, she had not fooled herself, for she had neither the headache nor any other malady; she merely wanted to be home in case the duke should call.

Again was she disappointed; for the only time the door to the drawing room opened was just before luncheon when Harriet came in to announce that she and the vicar were returned.

"My dear, Julia,'' she said, clasping her friend's hand, "you do recall what we spoke about yesterday, don't you? You do realize it is truly best you never see the duke again?''

"Of course!'' said Julia, attempting an air of unconcern.

"You were quite right to have warned me off any further association with him!"

So said Julia, very sensibly, but her heart could not have been more at odds with those rational words. She knew herself to be inexperienced in love, but she didn't think she had to be the recipient of too many kisses to know when a man was deeply attracted to her. Then she recalled that, aside from a few kisses, the duke had never given her any indication of his feelings. When she chanced to suppose that a man of his reputation had probably kissed a good many women in his time, and that none of those kisses had led to any greater bond, she was forced to realize that he had probably been flirting with her and nothing more.

All the many warnings Harriet and the vicar had uttered concerning the duke and his scandalous behavior came rushing back to Julia in one great sweeping wave. Under the force of such an assault, she found herself wavering. It was so much easier in his absence to believe him capable of the many scandalous deeds and misconducts that rumor laid at his doorstep. She was, she decided, better off having nothing to do with him. She was still telling herself so, and feeling her spirits sink appreciably, when she and the Clousters arrived at the village assembly rooms later that evening.

A swift glance about told Julia that the duke was not in attendance. Her spirits plummeted. She had hoped, quite unreasonably, that he would be there. To find him absent told her how right Harriet had been about him. He was not at all in love with her, she realized, or he would have made some sort of push to see her, if not at the card party or in the privacy of the drawing room at the vicarage, then at least in the very innocent surroundings of a village assembly.

Her enjoyment of the evening was quite ruined, but she put a brave face upon her distress and followed the

Clousters as they made their way about the perimeter of the dance floor toward a clutch of friends and acquaintances.

Harriet and her husband introduced Julia to a number of people; chief among them was young Mr. Worthing, the very same paragon Harriet had described the day before. He was indeed a very pleasing young man, and immediately upon his introduction to Julia, he begged the favor of the next dance.

Having accepted, she put her gloved hand in Mr. Worthing's when the music began and took her place on the dance floor. Throughout the next set, he did his best to engage her, smiled quite sunnily upon her and complimented her on the grace with which she executed her steps.

She knew he was striving to fix her interest; so, too, did she know that he appeared to be a very nice young man, indeed. But she found herself thinking instead that the Duke of Warminster had a more charming smile by half and that she was much more flattered by the attention the duke had shown her than she was by Mr. Worthing's compliments.

Still, she smiled and danced with Mr. Worthing, ever mindful of the promise she had made to Harriet that she would have nothing more to do with the duke and that she would instead devote her energies to securing a husband.

"You should feel very well gratified, my dear Julia," said Harriet in a lowered voice some time later. "I see Mr. Worthing has not been from your side all evening except for those instances when you were compelled to dance with another. Tell me, my dear: Do you like him? Is he not the very gentleman you described to me as your ideal in a husband?"

Julia felt herself flush and wished most heartily that she had never confided such things to Harriet. "I wish you would not speak so!" she hissed, urgently.

"Very well, I shall not tease you! The color in your cheeks

tells me all I need know! And it very much appears Mr. Worthing means to fix his interest with you, as well!"

"Harriet, please! Mr. Worthing has given no indication of any such thing!"

"There is a way to discover his intentions, you know. If he contrives to find some way to take you a little apart from the crowd," said Harriet, sagely, "you shall know he means to court you. Mark my words!"

Her prediction quickly bore itself out. Attracted by the sound of their whispered exchange, Mr. Worthing smiled down upon Julia. "May I offer you a glass of lemonade, ma'am? I should be happy to fetch one for you, or if you'd like to refresh yourself a little, I could simply accompany you to the punch table," he said, offering her his arm.

Julia knew what was expected of her. She slipped her hand through the crook of his elbow and, fully mindful of Harriet's prophecy, allowed herself to be led away from the dancing guests to a smaller room where drinks and light refreshments were being served.

She should have been gladdened by the prospect that she had been singled out to receive the attentions of a most pleasing young man. She should have been gratified to find that the first stage of her plan to remarry, and thereby secure her future, had been so easily fulfilled. Instead, Julia felt only a deep sense of disappointment. She was being courted by a man of sense and dependability; she would rather have been courted by the Duke of Warminster.

She forced a smile to her lips and accepted a glass of lemonade from Mr. Worthing. She had taken her first tentative sip when she heard a well-loved voice behind her, saying, "Good evening, Lady Pettingale."

She almost choked on her lemonade. Turning quickly, she found Gavin standing there, looking quite handsome in evening dress. She set her glass clattering down on the table and, visibly distracted, said, "So, you came after all!" She perceived that he was watching her, an odd little smile playing at his lips, and felt unaccustomedly flustered. His smile grew as she stammered, "I mean to say, I didn't know you were in the neighborhood . . . When you didn't call at the vicarage, I thought you had . . . not that I wished you to call, of course!"

"Perhaps you would be good enough to introduce me to your companion," he said mildly.

"Of course! Gavin, this—this is Mr. Worthing!"

Gavin shook Worthing's hand and said, "I believe this dance was promised to me. I shall return Lady Pettingale to you presently, if she so wishes."

He tucked Julia's suddenly trembling fingers into the crook of his arm and led her back into the assembly room.

Immediately upon their entrance, Julia found the eyes of the other guests upon them, forcibly bringing to mind yet again the many warnings she had been given concerning the duke. Most notably did she recall Harriet's caution that her reputation would sink past redemption if she were to be seen in his company.

She blurted out urgently, "I-I do not wish to dance with you!"

"No? Very well, then. Shall we sit down here, instead?" Still claiming her hand, he led her over to where a pair of chairs were situated apart from the others.

"I would rather you returned me to Mr. Worthing!"

"Why? What has he—? Oh, I see how it is!" he said, the light of understanding in his eyes. "He must be the lucky bachelor who has tumbled into your trap."

She felt her face color. "Mr. Worthing is a very respectable young man—"

"And you mean to marry him, if you can," interpolated the duke. "You told me so once. You didn't mention him in particular, but some man very much like him. Is he as boring as I promised you he would be?"

"More so!" she said, seeing not the least bit of humor in his question.

His eyes searched her face. "From the way you are behaving, I could think you don't wish to see me. What is it? What has occurred to make you so wary of me?"

"Nothing!" she said, unable to meet his eyes.

"Less than the truth, Julia? That is not like you. Go on, tell me!" he said, compellingly. "Has that friend of yours been sharing with you more tales about me?"

"No! Well, rather, she has—but nothing worse than any of the other stories I already heard about you!"

"Then what?" he demanded.

She cast a nervous glance about the room and saw that their retreat to a secluded corner had not gone unnoticed by the other guests, nor had Harriet and her husband failed to notice their *tête-à-tête*. They hurried toward Julia and Gavin; a look of distress marred Harriet's face, and an expression of anger lined the face of the vicar.

Julia rose to her feet, determined to fend off any recriminations, but she discovered very quickly that their anger was not directed at her. Indeed, the vicar said in a low but angry tone, "Warminster! I should have suspected you capable of this kind of behavior!"

One of Gavin's dark brows flew up challengingly as he slowly got to his feet. "Speaking with a friend is hardly cause for recrimination, Clouster. Where did you learn your party manners?"

"Never mind my manners! Have a care for your own! You know very well you should not be speaking with Julia!"

"Once again you have flown to the wrong bait, Clouster. Lady Pettingale and I were simply sharing a few words of conversation in a public assembly. What could be more innocent?"

"You know very well that no young lady's reputation can weather an acquaintance with you," said the vicar, as Harriet wrapped a protective arm about Julia's shoulders. "Unless you have some more honorable intentions toward Julia, I suggest you behave as a gentleman and bow out, Warminster. Well? What is it to be?"

Julia cast a pensive glance toward Gavin. Her eyes met

his, and in their dark depths, she detected no evidence of a man about to declare himself. Her heart sank.

If he cared for her, now was the time to say it; if his intentions were honorable, nothing would have prevented his saying so.

In vain did she wait for his answer; instead, his silence was more eloquent than any protests he might have made. So! His intentions were not honorable, after all! She should have been glad to have discovered such a truth before she had made any greater mistake where he was concerned. She was, however, far from glad. Her heart sank, and she felt quite close to tears.

The vicar nodded his head wisely, saying, "I thought as much. Be good enough, if you please, to keep your distance from Julia from this day on."

So saying, he escorted Julia and Harriet out into the summer evening. Julia was feeling quite low when she climbed up into Clouster's vehicle, little aware of anything that was happening about her.

As the carriage headed back toward the vicarage, Harriet looked at her with a worried expression and patted her hand consolingly, saying, "My dear, I had no notion the duke would behave in such a manner! And at a public assembly, too! When I saw that he had spirited you away to a secluded corner, I could scarce believe it. Such affrontery! How horrid the entire episode must have been for you, my dear!"

Harriet continued to speak so for the next several minutes while Julia blessed the darkened shadows of the carriage. She felt very close to tears and dared not trust herself to speak. It was a difficult lesson, she knew, to discover that the man she loved did not return her regard. To have learned it in front of Harriet and her husband was quite the bitterest of pills. Vividly did she recall the times she had championed the duke. How naïve she had been! How stupid!

She was consumed by such thoughts as the carriage

bowled along toward the vicarage. Vaguely, Julia was aware of Harriet's voice droning on and on for a good portion of a mile. She only noticed that Harriet had stopped talking when she heard her gasp slightly.

Julia looked at her friend and saw that Harriet's expression had frozen into one of horrified surprise and that her attention was riveted on something outside the window of the carriage.

Julia leaned forward to follow Harriet's gaze. In the moonlight she could discern a small rise some distance away, and atop it was a figure on horseback, watching the progress of their carriage as it made its way along the lane.

Her heart leapt within her breast. She recognized him immediately, of course. It was the Duke of Warminster who sat so imposingly astride his mount. Her breath caught as she waited to see what, if anything, he would do.

He didn't keep her waiting long. As Julia watched from the carriage, he set his horse in motion. The spirited animal caricoled slightly, then set off pall-mall down the rise on a direct course for their carriage.

In an instant he was on the road before them, forcing them to a halt. Gracefully, he slipped from his saddle and flung open the carriage door.

He cast a cursory glance toward Harriet and her husband; then, wordlessly, he held out his hand toward Julia.

Her lips went dry, and she flicked her tongue nervously over them. She didn't dare look at Harriet or at the vicar, for she knew what she would see on their faces: shock, disapproval, horror. They would be stunned to see that she even hesitated instead of rejecting the duke's gesture outright.

She didn't look at them. She looked only at the duke, searching for some sign that would tell her what she wanted to know; that would convince her she was right to follow her heart instead of letting her prim-and-proper head dictate her actions.

Slowly, tentatively, she stretched out her hand toward

his, but some remaining scruple caused her to stop just short of touching him. She looked, unblinking, into his eyes, willing him to say something—*any*thing—that would help her make up her mind.

He obliged by gruffly saying, "Julia Pettingale, I'm a bounder and a cad. I can give you a dozen reasons why you shouldn't marry me, and you can probably give me a dozen more."

She found her voice. "Are . . . are you *asking* me to marry you?"

Almost he denied it. Almost he succumbed to that nagging doubt that said any marriage proposal he might offer Julia Pettingale would only end in rejection. He wouldn't go through that; he wouldn't be able to bear losing her. But if he didn't pose the question, he knew she would be lost to him forever. He steeled himself and said, "Yes, I'm asking you to marry me."

She didn't realize she had been holding her breath, but she must have been, for she gave a great sigh of laughing relief and placed her hand in his.

"Julia! You cannot do this!" uttered Harriet, aghast.

The vicar was more direct. "Julia, I forbid you to get down from this carriage! I'm shocked to think you would even entertain such a proposal! You're a willful, shameless girl!"

"You are speaking of the woman I intend to marry," said the duke warningly. "I could call you out for that, Clouster."

"But you won't," said Julia, stepping neatly down from the carriage. "I shall not care what he may call me now, for I know that one day very soon he shall call me your wife."

"Very soon, indeed," agreed the duke, and his expression softened. "In the meantime, I'm taking you to your father, Julia."

"My . . . my father?" she repeated, stunned. "But he disowned me! He wants nothing to do with me!"

"On the contrary, he wants very much to see you. He loves you and misses you."

She cast him a dazzling look. "My father wants to see me? But how . . . ? Somehow I am sure I shall have you to thank for this!"

"Don't start adorning me with hero qualities. I had to see you restored to your father unless I wished to marry a penniless widow."

She laughed happily. "When shall I see him?"

"I can have you there tomorrow, if we make a start for it first thing in the morning."

The reverend scowled. "And what do you intend to do until morning?" he demanded.

"Have no fear, Clouster, we'll observe the proprieties. I'll take good care of Julia."

"Why should I believe you?" demanded the vicar. "Why should I take the word of a man of your repute? Why should I think you will treat Julia any differently than you have treated countless women in the past?"

"Because I love her." Gavin said the words quietly, and when he was done, he was rather surprised to realize how easily they had come to him. He decided to say them again, but this time, he clasped both of Julia's hands in his and looked into her eyes. "Because I love you."

It took her a moment to find her voice. "And I love you."

He didn't need to hear anything more. In one strong, swift movement he lifted her in his arms and set her on the back of his horse. Then, just as he had on another occasion, he climbed up behind her and wrapped his arms about her to draw her against the strength of his body.

Looking down, Julia could see Harriet's face go red. "Julia! Julia Pettingale, you cannot go off like that! Why, it's—it's positively indecent!"

Julia ignored this stricture and said instead, "Goodbye, dear Harriet. Thank you for letting me come to stay with you. You must call at Merrifield and visit me. Soon, I hope!"

"But not too soon," said the duke, with a pointed look that revived the color in Harriet's cheeks. He swung his mount about and set off toward home. But he didn't travel very far before he felt an urgent need to bring his horse to a halt and kiss Julia quite thoroughly.

When he was done, he looked down into her face, raised so charmingly and innocently toward his. He felt a niggling of conscience and asked, "Are you very certain about this, Julia? There's still time to change your mind, still time to do the right thing and go back to the vicarage with your friends."

"I *am* doing the right thing," she said with certainty.

"But my reputation—you heard for yourself what Clouster said about me and my women."

"Petty rumors," she pronounced. "What do I care for them?"

One of his dark brows flew to a challenging angle. "Is it possible? Are you the very same Julia Pettingale I met earlier this week, a woman who spouted respectable phrases and adjured me to have a care for my reputation?"

She smiled that half-smile that warned him he was about to be charmed. "Indeed, I am," she said, raising her lips very invitingly toward his. "But I have decided that I should like to have a scandalous reputation of my own—one that shall rival yours. What do you say to that?"

He smiled slightly. "I say you have come to the right teacher," he said.

And then he tightened his arms about her and kissed her wholeheartedly.

WATCH FOR THESE ZEBRA REGENCIES

WATCH FOR THESE REGENCY ROMANCES

LOOK FOR THESE REGENCY ROMANCES